The Witch Squad

A Witch Squad Cozy Mystery: Book #1

M.Z. Andrews

ISBN-10: 1542403901
ISBN-13: 978-1542403900

DEDICATION

To my mother.
You believed in my writing before I could even print my
own name. For that, I thank you.
All my love and appreciation,
M.Z.

CHAPTER ONE

"We are the delinquents, the misfits, the deliciously enchanted souls of this human realm; we are the gypsy warriors of the Earth – reckless incarnations of the true soul of every wanderer of this life. It is within the boundaries of this seminary that we submit to the development of our craft. We call upon the magic within these hallowed walls to sharpen our senses and direct our energy. Let the golden lamp light our doorways for the seemingly misguided, may we forever guide them to a truer calling and a higher purpose."

My tiny beater car wheezed heavily with annoyance as I braked long enough to roll down my window and read the quote on the plaque at the entrance of the all-girls boarding school.

Touted as a reformatory for troubled "special" women, my mother preferred to refer to this stint as "finishing school." I, on the other hand, was much more keenly observant and realistic. If one didn't want to mince words, I was being shipped off to witch boarding school.

So there it is. I'm a witch. Consider yourself special. I admit to few people that I'm a witch. I've learned that it just doesn't pay to be honest. Honesty gets you a trip to the principal's office and promptly from there an overnight visit to a psychiatric unit. No, I've had enough with the honesty crap, which is probably how I began my addiction to lying – which progressed to cheating and then eventually, stealing, and thus, how I found myself in the situation I'm currently in.

The warm scent of fall breezed in my open window and encircled my long, auburn hair, sending it cascading around my shoulders in tumultuous waves. The rustle of dried leaves at the end of the long winding driveway could be heard out the window.

"At least it's a beautiful autumn day," said the voice next to me.

I turned to look at the woman sitting in the passenger seat. An older reincarnation of myself, she had the same delicate features I had – a tiny little nose, delicate hands, and the same radiant green eyes, but her hair no longer spun the same reddish hue that mine did. Instead, it was laced with too many white strands to count. Courtesy of me, I was sure, she'd claim.

"A beautiful day for whom, Mother? Certainly not me! You get rid of your only daughter today. I bet you can't wait to get home and have the whole house to yourself. I suppose you're going to be throwing a 'got-rid-of-Mercy-party' the second you get home," I surmised angrily as I rolled up my window to stop my long hair from knotting anymore than it already had.

My mother looked at me sternly. "Mercy, I certainly am not looking forward to 'getting rid of you' as you so delicately put it. Why would I want you to go? You're my best friend. It kills me that you're leaving me."

I peered at her out of the corner of my eye. She certainly didn't look like she was losing her best friend. "If that's true then let's just turn the car around and head on home," I suggested with a hurt-filled voice.

"You know I would allow that if I could Mercy. But the courts have ordered you to get outside help. We both know what kind of outside help you need. This finishing school will serve you well and then you'll come home!"

I rolled my eyes at my mother as my car chugged loudly along the driveway, passing through a large standing of mature red oak trees. "Quit calling it finishing school, Mother! I'm not a young lady being prepped for entrance into some elite society. Let's be real here. I'm a witch who's gone off the rails."

My mother sighed and slumped back in her seat. We sat in silence as we made our way to the entrance of the Paranormal Institute for Witches or just The Institute as it was called on the street.

The Institute was a small school, located on the outskirts of Aspen Falls, Pennsylvania, a small community nestled snuggly in the heart of the Appalachian Mountains. We'd trekked quite a distance to reach The Institute, but it was the only school for paranormals my mom could find anywhere near our hometown of Dubbsburg, Illinois.

The long driveway came to a fork in the road. A large hand painted sign stood before us. A silhouette of a witch holding a broomstick pointed right, a silhouette of a wizard holding a starred wand pointed left, and the driveway up the center was marked Staff Entrance Only. I pulled the steering wheel to the right and cruised forward onto the campus.

I was vaguely surprised to see several handfuls of students and their families unloading their cars in the drop off zone. People had brought television sets, rolled carpets, futons, mini refrigerators, and microwaves. I looked into the backseat at my rolling suitcase, my backpack, and my garbage bag filled with the rag quilt my granny had sewn me when I was 10. I suddenly wondered if I had under packed for the occasion.

"I told you we should have packed you some comforts of home," my mother chided as we drove past the unloading zone and into a parking lot. The sign next to the parking lot read, 'Witch parking only, all others will be toad,' and it had a little picture of a witch's broom leaning against the words.

Oh my god. I mouthed to myself as I swung the car

into the nearest empty space. Mom gave my hand a little squeeze before jumping out of the car and grabbing the garbage bag from the backseat and slamming the door shut.

I grabbed my keys, cell phone and wallet from the center console and got out of the car to pull my suitcase and backpack from the back seat. Mom watched as I extended the handle on my suitcase and threw the backpack around my shoulders.

"Need any help Mercy?" she asked as she started forward towards the school.

"Nope, I've got it, Mother," I sighed dramatically.

Standing before the imposing sandstone building that would be my home for the next two years gave me pause. Few things in life intimidated me, so I wouldn't want to use that word, but something about the dark shadows the building cast across the sprawling campus made my heart lodge in my throat momentarily.

"It's going to be okay, Merc," my mother said as she retraced her steps back towards me. I allowed her to link arms with me and together we made our way through the parking lot.

In the unloading zone, a heavyset girl in a bright cotton sundress was loading a rolling cart with an enormous array of kitchenware from her car. The girl looked up at me as I walked by her. Our eyes met for a split second – she looked like she was just about to shoot me a smile – before I looked away. I didn't need any of that smiling crap. No first day of school besties for me. I was a loner, and I'd always be a loner.

In my previous life, as a paranormal being in a school of, well, normal beings, I didn't exactly make a ton of friends. So I'd done the opposite my whole life. I'd made enemies. I had never even given anyone the ability to get close to me. Why would I start now?

Mom and I breezed into the school unceremoniously and stopped at the folding table at the bottom of the stone staircase. A trio of women were chatting excitedly as we approached them.

"Hello! Welcome to the Paranormal Institute! May I have your last name, please?" the youngest of the three women asked me cheerfully, her nametag read Brittany Hobbs.

I shot my mother a disgusted look. I couldn't stand cheerful people. They were just so...cheerful. "Habernackle," I said expressionlessly. "Mercy."

"It's a pleasure to have you here Mercy Habernackle," she cooed as she found my name on the list on her clipboard. "And who did you bring with you today?"

What were we? In Kindergarten? "This is Linda," I said dryly.

"Well, hello, Linda, are you Mercy's mother?"

Mom nodded. I could feel the tense energy radiating off of her. These people were already annoying her as well. "Yes I am, is this where we pick up her room key?"

The woman smiled, flashing us a set of pearly white perfectly straight teeth. "Well yes, it is! Mercy, you're in room 215. You just take these stairs here and take a left down the hallway, and you'll find your room. Here's your room key," she handed me a lanyard with a key attached as well as an ID badge. "This is your meal card and ID for all Institute events. There is a family cookout at noon in the courtyard. You're both invited to attend!"

"Great," I croaked and pulled the lanyard over my head and down around my neck. "Let's go Mom."

I grabbed my bag and Mom and I began our ascent up the wide curved stone staircase. I peered into each doorway as we walked down the hallway. In each room girls from about 17 to their early twenties were unpacking. Tile floors, stone walls, and metal bunk beds made the rooms feel cold. We had to step over a big roll of carpet as we made our way further down the hall. I watched the numbers on each room, and when I came to room 215, I had to check the number twice. My room didn't look like the rest of the rooms with a tile floor and stone walls.

I eyed the room across the hallway. Tile floor, stone walls, metal bunk bed. Then I peered back into room 215. Wall to wall plush carpeting in a mottled grey covered the tile floor. The stone walls were covered with movie posters, the window was topped with an aqua valance, and the top bunk of the metal bunk bed had a grey and aqua chevron bedding set with matching grey furry throw pillows and a stuffed aqua colored owl. It looked like a Pottery Barn had exploded in my dorm room.

My mouth hung open as I entered the room. The wall behind the door had a small aqua colored futon sofa, and there was a mini fridge in the corner with a little microwave on top of it. Next to it was a small kitchen cart with clear plastic drawers and it looked like the drawers were full of snack foods and kitchen utensils.

"What in the world?" my mother asked, as thoroughly bewildered as I was feeling.

"Did you spring for the deluxe accommodations or what?" I asked her unenthusiastically. "Because I think you should ask for your money back. This place is giving me a toothache."

Suddenly we heard a squeal coming from the doorway. We turned to look and a girl who looked to be a couple of years younger than me, dressed in *the most* clichéd witches outfit I had ever seen was standing in the doorway with her hands clasped together. "Oh my! Mercy Habernackle?" she asked.

I nodded with my mouth agape. She was a tiny girl – a pixie would likely dwarf her – she wore a pair of green and purple striped leggings with a matching purple mini skirt over them and black pointy-toed high heeled boots. Her top – if you could call it a top – was purple as well and barely served to cover her tiny breasts. Her abs were left uncovered, and I could see why. She was extremely fit, and for a brief moment, I found myself a wee bit jealous of her six pack abs. I suddenly wished I hadn't quit gymnastics when I turned 13. The girl's short hair was dyed a bright orangey-red, and she topped off the whole ridiculous outfit with a big, wide-brimmed black witch's hat. You know, the ones that little kids wear for Halloween when dressing up as a witch, but real witches in the 21st century would never actually be caught dead in.

I looked around and suddenly wondered if I was being punked. Was a camera team going to jump out of my closet? This had to be a joke. This couldn't possibly be my, *gulp*, roommate, could it?

The girl approached me and before I knew what was happening, she'd taken the items in my arms from me and set them on the floor. Then in a flash I found her skinny little arms thrown around my neck. "It's such a pleasure to meet you, Mercy! I'm your roommate Jax!"

I stood there, stiff as a board, allowing her minute frame to engulf me in what a normal person would appreciate as an affectionate hug. I, on the other hand, did not appreciate affectionate hugs, nor did I generally tolerate them, but this one had caught me off guard. When I finally became aware of what was happening, I ducked my head to remove my unwanted witch necklace and set her promptly down on her feet.

"Not really a hugger," I said gruffly.

"Oh, it's alright, I'm enough of a hugger for the both of us," she chirped, her bright blue eyes twinkling.

My head began to throb as I suddenly felt panic sweep through my body. First the smiling girl in the driveway, next the painfully cheerful camp counselor in the entrance, then the sticky sweet dorm room, and now this – an uber annoying pixie for a roommate. Could the college experience *be* any worse?

I shot my mother a panicked look. She closed her eyes and exaggeratedly inhaled a deep breath through her nose. I knew that was her signal for me to do the same. I nodded and closed my eyes and inhaled my own deep breath and counted to ten.

.

CHAPTER TWO

"So what do you think of the room, roomie?"

I swallowed hard and looked around. The urge to vomit hit me like a Mack truck and I had to swallow hard a few more times to make sure my breakfast didn't hit the furry rug. "It's sure...something," I growled through gritted teeth.

"Isn't it? I spent the whole summer planning it out perfectly," Jax shared excitedly.

My mother shot me a warning glance. *Be nice.*

"Mmmhmm. Yeah, it's sure...cute," I spat. I despised cute.

"Isn't it, though?" she purred. "I emailed you a couple of times at the beginning of summer so we could coordinate our stuff, but I must have been given the wrong email address because I never got a response. I hope you're okay with the colors I've chosen for us."

I bit my bottom lip and tried really really hard not to

explode. I had hoped that witches would be more like me – a moody bunch with a penchant for the dark and dreary. I was very disappointed to find out they were more like an advertisement for the Gap.

"Oh yeah, I just love aqua, it's seriously, my fave," I tossed out with fake enthusiasm.

Jax's eyes lit up. "You do? Ohhhh, see! I just knew it was all going to work out. We're going to be lifelong friends; I just know it!"

I turned around to face the window and rolled my eyes. With that out of my system, I turned back around again and stared at Jax for a long moment. I could tell she wanted me to say something encouraging. "This is my mom, Linda," I finally said and hitched my thumb towards my mother who had finally sat down the garbage bag in her arms and begun to unpack it.

"Hi Mom," Jax squealed and rushed my mom to give her a big squeeze around her middle.

I couldn't help but roll my eyes again. She was like the annoying little sister that I never had, nor ever wanted.

Suddenly a loud bang followed by a scream filled the empty spaces of our room. Looking into the hallway, I saw the two girls from across the hall bolt out of their room and chase the sound down the corridor. I poked my head out into the hallway and saw a curvy blonde in a crop top and booty shorts exiting her room waving her arms around through a cloud of black billowing smoke. A tall, thick, brunette followed her out of the room, coughing. Her face and body was covered in a thick layer of soot.

"What the heck, Holly?" the dark haired girl barked as she wiped the black soot off of her face. The whites of her eyes stood out from the black chalky mask around them, giving her the appearance of an alert black cat.

Several of the girls that had gathered in the hallway were covering their mouths, trying desperately not to laugh.

"What happened here?" asked a deep male voice from the other end of the hallway. As the smoke thinned I made out a short stout man wearing a blue jumpsuit. He carried a mop and was dragging a bright yellow squeaky bucket behind him.

The ponytailed blonde, apparently called Holly, looked at the floor sheepishly. "Sorry," she said more to herself than to him. "Accident."

"What kind of accident results in black smoke?" he gnarled. With his jaw set firmly, everyone could see that he was obviously angry with her.

She shrugged her shoulders. "I picked up my books from the bookstore. I-I was reading ahead."

He growled at her as he passed her by, but continued walking towards my end of the hallway. "Open a window! And clean up this mess!" He walked past me, shooting me a venomous look. The lights in the hallway bounced off of his scalp where his hairline had receded and suddenly he reminded me of a young Danny DeVito in Taxi, a show whose reruns played incessantly in my house because of my mother's obsession with Marilu Henner. His name tag read Seymour H. I wondered why Seymour H. was a custodian in an all girls' school if he so obviously didn't like girls. Seymour and his squeaky cart made his way to the end of the hall and unlocked the janitor's closet to stow away his gear before disappearing down the stairs I had just come up.

Once Seymour was out of sight, the girls who had congregated in the hallway to gawk began to retreat one by one.

The brunette didn't budge as she stared at her arms and soot covered clothing. "Look at me, Holly!" she hollered incredulously to her roommate.

Holly cowered. The brunette was at least six inches taller and probably had 60 pounds on the smaller girl. "I'm sorry Alba, I didn't mean to…"

Alba's face remained unchanged by the apology. I wasn't sure if it was because she didn't accept the apology or if that was just her face. Either way, I appreciated Alba's temperament. That was the kind of person I had been hoping to find at witch school.

I went back to my room and after one quick glance around I decided I had to get out of there. "Let's go eat lunch Mom?" I suggested.

Mom nodded and cocked her head towards Jax, who was busy color coding the hanging clothes in her small closet. I knew she wanted me to invite the little thing, but I didn't think I could handle her cheerfulness while I ate my lunch. I shook my head and scowled at her.

"Jax, I'm going to take my mom to lunch and then say goodbye to her, I'll catch up with you later."

Jax turned around and gave me a brief flicker of a pair of sad eyes before she quickly recovered and nodded her head. "Oh, you're leaving so soon Mom? I sure hope I'll see you again soon! Don't be a stranger."

Mom gave her a tiny smile. "Illinois is pretty far away, I'll probably just send for Mercy at Christmas time. I'm sure I'll see you again someday though. Have a nice school year, Jax."

Jax threw her arms around my mother's middle again, hugging her tightly. I suddenly wondered if Jax had a mother of her own. Maybe I'd get around to asking her that someday. For now, I had to get out of the room.

Mom and I quietly left my room and headed down the stairs to the stark stone lobby. A small handful of girls and their mothers were still checking in as we followed the big signs to the outdoor commons area where the family luncheon would soon take place.

"You really don't have to stay for lunch, Mom," I told her, biting the inside of my cheek to keep from displaying any real emotion.

"You don't want me to stay?" My mother's face was glum as I leaned back against one of the large scarlet oak trees in the courtyard.

The smoky scent of a charcoal barbecue swirled around me, causing my stomach to churn suggestively. I kicked at an unearthed tree root with the toe of my black Chuck Taylor high-tops and did what I always did – pretended like I didn't care. Being hard and mean was so much easier than caring.

"It's really not necessary at all. I'm 19 years old and you're dropping me off at college. I don't need Mommy around anymore." I bit on the inside of my cheek harder as my eyes threatened to well up with tears at any moment.

I could tell my mother wasn't having as much luck fighting her emotions. As the first tears began to cascade down her soft rosy cheeks, she reached her arms out in front of her and pulled me into a tight embrace.

I tried not to squeeze her back. I tried to be tough, but when I felt the coolness of her tears touch my skin, I felt a shift inside of me. It was as if I suddenly realized I was saying goodbye to my childhood. In this precise moment. This was it. Even though I'd officially reached adulthood over a year ago, this was the moment I said goodbye to being a kid and began my life as an adult and in addition, this was the moment I said goodbye to my mother. My one and only lifelong best friend.

The realization hit me like lightning and for that tiny moment in time, I allowed myself to feel the real emotion of the situation. I hugged my mom tightly and let my cheek rest on her shoulder, the tears came as if they'd been loitering there – just waiting for the nod of approval before falling. And fall they did, in reckless abandonment. In a way, it was a good feeling. It was cathartic and maybe I needed a little catharsis in my life. Maybe that was part of one of my many problems.

In another way, it was like I broke a barrier that had been there since I was a girl – it was that tough outer shell that I didn't let down for anything or anyone – the thought that somehow I had a flaw in my armor, caught me off guard. I suddenly realized my place, the situation, and that there may be other students around and I immediately disengaged myself from my mother.

With my face towards the mighty oak tree behind us, I lifted my black framed glasses and quickly used the sleeves of my well worn AC/DC sweatshirt to wipe away any traces of my breakdown. I could immediately tell by the smudges of black on my sweatshirt that I had smeared my eyeliner, the only makeup I wore on my face.

Ugh, great. I nervously peered around me, looking for any signs that anyone had seen me cry. Thankfully, no one was around.

Mom gave me a reassuring smile. "No witnesses, Merc. You're safe."

"Thank God." I gave her a half smile. "I'll miss you Mom," I told her honestly.

Mom's chin began to quiver. "How am I ever going to live without you Mercy? I miss you already."

I looked around once again. "You'll manage. You'll start to date. Maybe you'll take up a hobby."

Mom laughed through the tears that were falling again. "No one wants to date a dried up old witch like me."

I laughed despite myself and gave her a real hug. One last hug before she drove away and I didn't see her again until a holiday of some sort. "You're not dried up, Mom. And you're not old. You're what I like to call, vintage. Besides, you're still hot. Maybe you should get some Clairol and wash away the gray."

"They are white thank you, and I owe every last one of these to you, my sweet Mercy Bear."

I rolled my eyes. "Mercy Bear? Really Mother. I'm 19

years old. I think it's time you think of a new nickname for me now, don't you?"

Mom smiled at me adoringly and sniffed away her runny nose while dotting at her eyes with a tissue. "You're all grown up, that's for sure. Well, sweetheart, if you don't need me. I guess I'll get back on the road. I'm going to try and make it as far as Akron tonight."

"Ok, drive safe. Don't do any chanting and driving, you know how that's worked out for you in the past."

My mom's eyes rolled and she snorted out her nose at me. "I blame you for that."

"You blame me for everything, Mom."

She smiled. "Promise me you'll try hard Mercy. This school is a big deal. Your life is a big deal. I need you to focus your energy here. Work hard and then you can come home. Alright?"

I nodded. *I'll try, Mom.* I swallowed hard and gave her a little wave as she walked off towards the parking lot.

When she was halfway to the front driveway, she swiveled on her heel and turned back around to yell at me. "I love you Mercy!"

"Love you too, Mom."

CHAPTER THREE

I was the first one seated on the marble picnic benches at the family luncheon, so I got front row seats to the crazy train of families that had accompanied their students to school. The variety of people that had come to the Institute was wide.

It was easy to pick out the rich kids. They were dressed in designer clothes, had two parents along for the ride, and looked like they never scored below an A on anything in their perfect little lives.

There were a few poor kids, but not many, the school was too expensive for poor kids, but some had made it on scholarships. Those kids had mostly arrived by plane, as the school had flown them in. They came without family fanfare and many had already grouped themselves as they'd ridden together on the plane and then bus into Aspen Falls.

Then there were the bookworms, those who already

had their noses buried in books. And then there were the kids like me – somewhere between rich and poor. Not a book worm, but not completely clueless. We were scattered amongst the rest. Like little dandelions in a sea of sweet Kentucky Bluegrass.

Lost in thought while waiting for the show to get on the road, I was disengaged from my thoughts by the sound of an all too familiar saccharine voice. "Mercy! Mind if I join you?"

I looked up to see Jax's tiny little frame hustling towards me excitedly. *Ugh.*

"No, go ahead," I uttered, lowering my head in embarrassment that my roommate was dressed like that. I just knew people were going to think that we were both a joke. And then Mom's voice popped into my head, *Mercy Habernackle! Don't concern yourself with what other people think! Their opinions are not what matters. Your opinion is what matters.* Unfortunately, my opinion in this case, sided with other people.

Jax looked around. "Did Mom leave?" she asked, her bottom lip jutted out.

"Yeah, she needed to get going. She wants to try and make it as far as Akron before it gets dark."

"That's great she could drive you here," Jax said with a little tilt of her head. "Where are you from again?"

"Illinois. Dubbsburg. A little town outside of Chicago. You?"

"Mmm, I'm from all over," she shared cryptically. I could feel she was holding back on me, but I didn't care enough to ask more. "Are you hungry?"

I nodded and rubbed my stomach. "Ravenous. We had breakfast at 5 this morning and we didn't stop for a snack anywhere."

"It looks like lunch should start any minute," she said as we watched them bring out the side dishes from the dining hall and set them on a long buffet table.

I took a moment to look around the courtyard. It was a gorgeous place to be, if I were being honest. The colors of the trees over our heads were all the lovely shades of fall. The ground was covered with red cobblestone in a circular design and there were low sandstone walls, just high enough to sit on, partially enclosing the courtyard with openings at each of four sidewalk paths. One path led to Winston Hall, my dormitory, another path led to the front parking area, and there were two other paths that I didn't know where they led.

"Have you done much exploring yet?" I asked Jax.

She nodded and pointed to the path behind the buffet tables. "Yes. That sidewalk there leads to our classrooms and the one to the left there is to Warner Hall, the men's dormitory."

My eyes grew big. I had seen the sign on the way in that suggested there were wizards here, but I didn't know what to make of it. My mother had told me it was just a school for witches. "There are boy's dorms here? I thought this was a girl's only school?"

"Well, the Paranormal Institute encompasses both schools – one for witches and one for wizards. They keep us separated. So we won't have any classes with the men. But I think we do have socials and whatnot with them."

I wonder if my mother knew she was putting me in a co-ed environment. She hadn't said a word to me about the wizard side of things – it was quite possible she wasn't even aware that there would be guys here.

Suddenly a loud voice boomed from the full-size speakers hanging around the courtyard and our eyes all swiveled to the podium set up in the middle of the commons area.

"Good afternoon. Welcome to the Paranormal Institute for Witches!" the announcer said as excited applause filled the open air arena. The announcer was an extremely tall thin woman with a long, flowing white dress belted at the waist. Her straight white hair was long as well; it rippled down her back and ended just above the swell of her bottom. She was a beautiful woman, and despite the fact that she looked fairly young, I got the feeling that she was much older than she appeared.

"My name is Miss SaraLynn Stone. I am the Supreme Sorceress of the Paranormal Institute for Witches. You may call me Miss Stone or Sorceress Stone. I have been with the Institute for as long as I can remember. I'd prefer not to put a number on my years of experience, but let's just say I've been practicing the craft for longer than many of you have been alive." She paused briefly while chuckles could be heard. "I'd like to thank all the parents for bringing your daughters to our hallowed halls. Without you and the care you have for your young women, they would be nothing. Ladies, let's give your parents a warm round of applause in thanks."

Sorceress Stone led the room in a hearty round of

applause for the parents. As the clapping died down, she spoke again. "I would also like to thank our teachers and our staff. Without you, this school would be nothing. Please stand so that we may acknowledge all the good that you do."

A row of faculty and staff seated in the first two round marble tables next to the dorm entrance stood and waved at the crowd as the clapping resumed.

"We have so many things to teach these young women, so many ways to focus their energy and hone their skills and abilities. I simply cannot wait to get started!" She clapped her hands together with emphasis. "I don't want to delay their educations any longer. So, ladies, let's enjoy one last dinner with your loved ones and then let them say their final goodbyes. Students, at one o'clock there will be a quick assembly in the Winston Hall lobby and then you shall be released to your rooms until classes begin tomorrow morning. I shall see you at one o'clock."

Jax and I ate lunch together while she did about 98% of the talking. I mostly sat and nodded and threw in the occasional, "Oh really?" to hold up my end of the conversation. She was an exhausting girl, but I learned that she was what they called a legacy at this school. Most of the women in her family had gone to The Institute and she felt a lot of pressure to measure up. There were a few moments, only a few mind you, don't go thinking I was getting soft, where I actually felt for the girl. She seemed to be a genuinely nice person with a good heart, and obviously, she had her own life issues she was dealing with, but she was also genuinely annoying.

After lunch and all the parents had gone, the group of women gathered in the Winston Hall lobby as we were instructed by Sorceress Stone.

"Ladies, we have set up displays of the extra-curricular activities that we offer here on campus. You may sign up for as many as you would like. But I do encourage each of you to get involved. It will make your time here at the Institute most rewarding and memorable. Each organization has a current member or officer standing by to answer any of your questions and assist you in any way they can. Once you've had an opportunity to wander through the lobby and visit each station, you may have the rest of the afternoon to finish unpacking or to tour the campus and get yourselves acquainted with your home for the next two years. Dinner will be served promptly at 6:00 in the dining hall."

With that, she clapped her hands twice in the air and headed to the back of the hall. Her long dress trailed behind her, giving her the impression that she was floating across the marble tiled floor.

"Oooh! I want to join this one!" Jax cooed as we looked at the bright pink poster board that read Potion club.

I lifted one corner of my lip, wrinkled my nose and grunted. "Why?"

"Why not?" she gushed. "I love potions! And I love clubs!"

I rolled my eyes as we strolled to the next table. The girl standing behind the table gave us each a free pen and invited us to karaoke night on Friday. The chant club would have their first welcome party for new recruits. Of course, Jax wanted to join that one too.

"You like chants too?" I asked her with a little chuckle.

"Of course I do. All witches like chants. Don't you like chants?" she asked me incredulously. Like if I didn't like chanting I wasn't a real witch or something.

I shrugged. "Chanting is alright."

The next booth was a recreational sports club – Witches Broomery Golf. *If only I had brought my broomstick, shucks.* Of course, Jax wanted to join that too. She bent over to sign her name on the registration list, but I stopped her. "Jax, don't you feel like you might be over committing?"

She held a hand up to her mouth and sucked in a breath. "Is that a thing?" she asked nervously.

I nodded with wide eyes. "Yes. If you over commit you risk getting burned out. You don't want to get burned out right away do you?"

She shook her head reverently. "No, I certainly don't want to get burned out."

"Right. So you pick a *few* things to sign up for. Not all of them."

Jax nodded as if the words I had spoken were the supreme almighty word of witchcraft. "Yes, of course," she said quietly, setting the pen gently back down on the sign-up table. We walked along in silence for a few moments and then she asked me inquisitively, "What are you going to sign up for?"

I looked around the booths and sighed deeply. "I'm not exactly what you call a social person."

"I could tell," Jax admitted with a hint of melancholy in her voice. "But it's ok, I still like you. And we're still going to be lifelong friends."

The fact that Jax still wanted to be my friend despite my moodiness surprised me. I'd never known anyone who could see past my hard outer layer and want to be my friend despite the rough edges. I looked at her briefly. Her crazy red dyed hair bounced around her shoulders under her wide-brimmed black hat and her bright blue eyes beamed up at me. *What a nut.* But then it occurred to me. I was the nut where I came from. And I literally *hated* it when I was younger and people wouldn't give me a chance – I'd grown accustomed to it the older I got, but as a child that was really hard. The thought made me exhale a deep sigh of regret and caused me to throw one arm around Jax's shoulder. "You're alright, Jax," I told her with a little smirk.

"I am?" she asked, astounded.

"You are."

Her face lit up like a Christmas tree as we finished the loop around the lobby, stopping to check out the Animal Powers Club, the Nature's Healing Club and the Sisters of Witchcraft Sorority.

"Ooh, I want to join a sorority!" Jax said excitedly and signed up at the registration table.

"Why would you want to join a sorority?" I asked her.

"Sisterhood. That's what witches are all about – sisterhood and working together for the greater good."

I shook my head from side to side. "No, that's not what *all* witches are about. Didn't you ever watch cartoons when you were a kid? Every witch I ever saw lived in a secluded cottage in the woods. You never see a team of witches solving the world's problems, do you?"

Jax considered my words for a second and then threw her hands up. "Oh well. I want to make friends here."

At the end of the loop, we wandered back outside to the courtyard and found the two girls from down the hall that had set off the explosion in their room. The brunette girl was cleaned up. The two of them were arguing as we approached them.

"All I'm saying is you shouldn't be doing spells in our room," Alba snarled at the busty blonde angrily.

"Well, where else am I supposed to do my homework?" Holly asked petulantly.

Alba sighed and leaned back against the marble picnic table they were standing next to. "I don't know. The library?"

"The library isn't even open yet," she whined.

"That's because we don't have any homework yet. Classes don't start until tomorrow, so what are you worrying about?"

Holly shrugged and threw her hands on her hips. "I'm a slow learner; my parents said I needed to study hard."

"Studying hard doesn't mean doing experiments in our dorm room."

I walked towards the girls, hoping to break up the fight between them. "Hey, I'm Mercy," I said to Alba and stretched my hand out to shake hers. This wasn't something I'd normally do, introduce myself like this, but I felt like someone needed to stop them from making fools of themselves in the middle of the quad and I'd had a sense earlier that Alba might be a good match for me.

Alba took one look at my outstretched hand and lifted her nose at it. She crossed her thick arms and turned her back to me.

Immediately I felt my blood simmering. It was such a rare thing for me to put myself out there like that and to get less than no response – to get a snobbish response, burned my butt.

Holly turned to me. Her cheeks were flushed red, either from embarrassment or anger over the fight she was having with her roommate. "Hi Mercy, I'm Holly," she said and tried to reach her hand out to mine. When I didn't take it right away, Jax grabbed it instead.

"It's so nice to meet you Holly. I'm Jax," she said excitedly.

I took a moment to really look at the two girls from down the hall. For being so short, Holly was a voluptuous thing. She had enormous boobs that spilled out of her little v-neck t-shirt. She had a slim waist and a badonkadonk that I knew had to have taken quite a bit of magic to get stuffed in those skinny jeans. Her platinum blonde hair had been released from the ponytail she sported earlier and was light and curly around her shoulders. Her flawless makeup complimented her blue eyes perfectly. I quickly decided my hall neighbor was quite the Cosmopolitan girl.

Alba seemed to be almost the complete opposite. She

wore no makeup on her tanned face. Her dark hair and dark eyes gave her an ethnic look, though I couldn't readily guess what nationality her ancestors might have originated from. She was a thicker girl, or *sturdy*, as my mother would call her and she was taller than me by about an inch or two and I was 5'10. Her hair was pretty short, cut just below her ears giving her quite the butch chick appearance. While I had originally thought I would enjoy a person like that, I didn't particularly appreciate being snubbed by one.

"Hi Jax," Holly said, shooting me a nervous look while she shook Jax's hand.

"Where are you girls from?" Jax asked the two new girls.

Holly looked up at her roommate. "Umm, I'm from California. Alba, here, is from New York."

Alba shot Holly a set of squinted eyes and curled her lip at the girl. "I'm from New Jersey. Get it right."

"Oh, sorry, Alba," she apologized. Then she turned back to Jax and me. "She's from New Jersey. Where are you girls from?"

"I'm from all over," Jax said, using her apparent standard answer. "Mercy's from Illinois."

"Well, it's nice to meet you both. I think I'm going to work on cleaning up our room now. I sort of – made a mess in there earlier," Holly said, but before she could walk away, Alba spun on her heel and walked past Jax and me and back towards our dormitory.

When she was out of earshot, I put a hand aside my mouth and whispered to Jax and Holly, "Well she's certainly a delight."

Holly giggled. "She's not that bad. She's just mad because I covered our room in soot."

"Yeah, so, what's up with that?" I asked curiously.

Holly's broad smile lit up her blue eyes. "I was reading ahead in our book of incantations. I found one that was a Witch's Good Luck spell. And well – I'm a little on the klutzy side, so I decided to try it and bless our room. The spell said I was supposed to have a four leaf clover with me, but I didn't have one, I thought it might work without it. I guess I was wrong."

"Oops!" Jax giggled and looked at me with laughter in her eyes.

"Sounds like the spell didn't help with that klutzy thing," I whispered to myself.

CHAPTER FOUR

I had to wear my extra thick Red Hot Chili Peppers hoodie to Intro to Witchcraft the next morning. For some reason I woke up with ripples of chills running up and down my spine and I couldn't get warm to save my life. Maybe it was just the brisk autumn wind blowing through Aspen Falls or maybe it was 'the gift' that just kept giving – sending me a covert signal. I rolled my eyes. Being a witch had yet to be a fun type of gift. The type you'd actually sit on Santa's lap as a kid and *ask* to be given. No, it really was more of a curse – and I had always wondered who I'd pissed off in my former life to have been cursed in such a way. Mom always told me that one day I'd appreciate my gift, but as I'd yet to come into all of my powers, I only saw myself as different, and in a world where different was uncool, I hadn't grown my sense of appreciation yet.

The nice thing about the Paranormal Institute was that classes were small. No big college lecture halls for us. The school touted its small class size, individualized attention, and world class instructors. And to start things off in the right way, we were given Sorceress Stone as our first teacher of the day. She didn't look much different than she had the day before, though her dress was grey, not white today, it looked like she'd ordered it from the same Witch Crew catalog, just in a different color.

"Ladies, I want you to know just how very excited I am to get to be your mentor. The Institute is going to open up a whole new world to you. You'll be able to do things you've never dreamed of doing before coming. Many of you are legacy's – coming from a long line of witches and wizards before you. But there are a few of you who have received your powers from other sources. To each of you alike, I welcome you. Now, before we begin our first lesson, I thought we should probably get to know one another. So, let's introduce ourselves and tell a little something about ourselves and if you have an idea of what your specialty might be, feel free to share it. For some, I realize you may not know your specialty yet, and that's fine. That's part of what you'll be doing here at The Institute. We'll declare majors by the end of this year! So, let's start with you," she said and pointed towards a rather large girl in the front row. I immediately recognized her as the girl who had tried to smile at me when she was unloading her car the day before.

The girl's round face reddened, but she stood up and faced the class. "Hello, I'm Mildred Porter, but my friends and family call me Sweets," she let a little giggle escape. "My specialty is matchmaking. I've matched a few people in high school, but I came to The Institute because I'd like to start my own matchmaking business someday. My parents said I needed to go to college first, so here I am!"

"Ooh, it's been years since I've had someone majoring in matchmaking wandering our halls, how deliciously fun!" Sorceress Stone said, punctuating her excitement by clapping her hands together as I'd seen her do the day before in the assembly. "Do you have a special matchmaking chant that's been passed down in your family or what's your ritual for your matchmaking, if you don't mind me asking?"

Sweets shook her head. "It's actually more of a … recipe," she shared.

"A recipe, I see, like a potion?" Sorceress Stone clarified, nodding her head at the class as if we were little children.

"Mmm, no, more like cupcakes, truffles, ooh, chocolate cheesecake, that's my favorite." Sweets' eyes lit up as she listed some of her favorite recipes.

"Oh, I see, well that *is* deliciously fun then, isn't it!"

I couldn't help but join the class in a little chuckle, no matter how much I thought getting to know one another was for the birds.

"It's very delicious," Sweets admitted as she took her seat. "I bake a little love into every treat."

"Well, it's so nice to meet you Sweets, welcome to The Institute. How about *you* next."

I looked up and found the Sorceress' bony little finger pointed directly at me. Ugh, I hated this part of class. Uneasily, I stood up and adjusted my glasses to sit higher on my nose and pulled my thick zip-up sweatshirt tighter around my body as I felt another shiver zip down my spine. "I'm Mercy. I'm from Illinois. My mom is a witch, and I am a witch," I said and then plopped back down in my seat.

"Whoa whoa whoa, stand back up, Mercy dear," she drawled. "We'd like to know more about you than that. Heavens we are all witches, dear. How long have you known you were a witch?"

I took a deep breath and then stood back up again. "I've known I was a witch since I was about three. My mom says for awhile she thought I was just talking to imaginary friends, but then when I began to know things I shouldn't or say certain things, she knew I had to be talking to ghosts. So, yeah. I've actually run across other things I can do naturally, you know just here and there over the years, but being able to talk to ghosts was really my first real skill. I have no ability to summon them yet, though. I have no idea what I'll major in. Talking to ghosts for the rest of my life isn't exactly on my list of career goals."

"That's a great story, Mercy. I'm so pleased you decided to join us."

I sat back down in a huff. I hadn't *decided* to join them, the courts had *ordered* me to join them, but I didn't intend on sharing that information with these people. I peered hatefully around the room; I detested all those sets of eyes on me. Another shiver ran down my spine, and I wondered if maybe I just wasn't coming down with something. Both my arms and legs were pebbled with goosebumps that wouldn't go away.

The Sorceress moved on to the rest of the girls' introductions.

I learned that Alba was telekinetic. She came from a long line of telekinetic practitioners and her family ran a furniture moving business in Jersey, where their skills came in handy. She had also recently discovered that she had a touch of mind reading ability, though it only came in and out in spurts, and she hadn't learned to control it yet.

Holly, whose natural assets were front and center again this morning, had premonitions. Whether they were through dreams, through touching specific objects, or sometimes she'd even just be struck with a random premonition during the day. She was unable to control most of those premonitions, and she wanted to learn to summon those powers at her will. I wanted to add that I suspected she had a few skills as an enchantress as well, but I thought better of it.

"How about you?" Sorceress Stone's ice blue eyes rested curiously on Jax.

Jax sank slightly under the Sorceress' intent gaze but stood to face the class as well. She'd toned down the witch look by removing the black hat, but still, she wore green striped tights and her pointy black toed boots under a black and green striped dress. "I'm Jax. Umm, I've done some conjuring and some potion making. I do just a little bit of everything."

Sorceress Stone regarded her for a few seconds longer and then clucked her tongue before moving on to the last few girls in the class. Jax visibly shuddered as the Sorceress walked past her. I immediately got the sensation that Jax was hiding something.

Before I could give it any thought, the door to our classroom was thrown open and Hobbs, the woman who had greeted me and my mother when we'd checked in the day before walked in and strode directly over to Sorceress Stone. They spoke in hushed whispers for a few brief moments and then the woman left the room. Sorceress Stone moved back to the center of the class and clapped her hands.

The chills that I'd been having hit even harder and I found myself seated at my desk shaking. Jax turned and looked at me. "Are you alright? You don't look so good."

With my arms wrapped around myself, I rubbed both arms with my hands and nodded, my head shook involuntarily. "I-I-I'm j-j-just c-c-cold," I stuttered.

"You're getting sick, I'm sure of it," Jax whispered back. "Maybe I should take you to the infirmary."

Before I could respond, Sorceress Stone turned to the class again. "Students. We have an emergency situation. Something has happened in town."

Whispers broke out across the room.

"Ladies, please. This is a serious situation. The body of a girl from the local high school has been found dead."

Gasps filled the room as I continued to shake. I realized that my shaking likely had something to do with the discovery of a body. My body often served as a warning shot, telling me when I would be approaching an emergent situation.

"Girls, I have been summoned to the scene of the crime. Often times the local police will call me to consult on a case of high priority. There have been numerous cases where our paranormal abilities here at The Institute have assisted the Aspen Falls Police Department in finding the culprit in a variety of cases."

"What do you want us to do?" I heard Jax's voice call out to the front of the room.

The Sorceress took a moment to consider her options silently. Then she looked up at the small class and made up her mind immediately. "You'll come along."

I looked at Jax as my chills began to immediately subside. It was as if a switch had flipped inside of me; my body temperature returned to normal. The goosebumps I hadn't been able to shake since breakfast began to flatten into my usual smooth flesh.

"You feeling better?" she asked me in surprise.

I nodded and whispered back, "Yeah, I feel almost all better, that's so weird."

"Ladies! Did you hear what I said?" Sorceress Stone asked Jax and me pointedly.

"I'm sorry Sorceress, Mercy wasn't feeling well. I thought I was going to have to take her to the infirmary for a moment, but she's suddenly looking better."

Our teacher looked down her long thin nose at me for just a moment. "Yes, well, she looks fine to me. Alright, get your things together. We're taking an impromptu field trip."

By the noise from around the room, it was obvious the rest of the students were excited to go.

"This is a very serious field trip, however. This isn't pumpkin picking at the local farmer's patch. This is a serious police investigation. Anyone not treating it as such will be reprimanded and not allowed to go again. You will be there with your eyes and ears only. Your mouths will stay shut – there will be no talking. There will be no asking questions. There will simply be you there, learning about the best way that you, as a paranormal individual, may assist law enforcement in the successful apprehension of a criminal. Are there any questions?"

Without my knowledge, my hand rose.

"Yes, Mercy?"

"What if we see a clue or our abilities perk up in some way that can help?"

Sorceress Stone's thin lips curled into a small smile. "Mercy, dear. I'm sure that anything you or the rest of the class picks up on, I will pick up on as well. If for some reason, I miss something, then you may report back to me when we return to the confines of The Institute. But under no circumstances will you impede a police investigation as a student of my institution. Is that clear?"

I didn't know what to say. I hadn't wanted to ask that question. Something inside of me asked that question without my consent, and now she was looking at me as if I were going to be a pain in her bony little butt.

"Yes, ma'am," I finally conceded, as heat filled my cheeks.

CHAPTER FIVE

I felt like a clown in a clown car as the whole class piled out of the school's old white van on the side of the heavily wooded road. The trees were an amazing assortment of reds, oranges, and yellows, but we didn't get the opportunity to enjoy the colors as we approached the flashing lights on the squad car. The hairs on my arms immediately stood on end as we neared the figure on the ground, draped in a dark colored tarp. It felt as if a force were pulling me closer to her as if she wanted me to save her. I looked at the other girls and wondered if they felt the same energy drawing us in.

An officer was standing over her body with a little notepad in his hands. Several other officers were directing the traffic, and the one in charge immediately greeted us as we approached the scene.

"Miss Stone, thank you for coming down here so quickly," the police officer said, shaking her hand. He eyed the group of us curiously.

"Detective Whitman, I appreciate you calling us. You know we are willing to help in whatever way we can. I hope you don't mind, I've brought my new group of students. We were in the middle of class when I got word of what had happened. These types of gruesome occurrences don't happen every day, and I decided I may as well get as many teachable moments out of them as possible."

He nodded seriously. "Indeed. Ladies, I will ask you to hang back for now, beyond the tape. Please don't touch anything at all," he advised us. "If you'll follow me, Miss Stone, right this way."

Sorceress Stone looked back at us as she followed him quickly over the police tape and into the thick of the investigation. Her eyes spoke volumes, and we knew to stay put and stay out of their way.

"My goodness, this would be a scary place to be killed, I can't even imagine!" Sweets said with a little drawl apparent in her voice.

"Where are you from Sweets," I asked her.

"Georgia, why?" she asked.

"No reason, I just thought I heard a bit of a southern accent."

"Yes, ma'am, Witch by birth, Southern by the grace of God," she smiled at me.

"You've never said that before, have you?" I laughed as I rolled my eyes at her little saying.

"You know I think my parents sent me to college in Pennsylvania to escape all the crime and murders in the city," Alba said. Her dark eyes glowed as she watched the crime scene investigation underway. "Who would have thought, little old Aspen Falls, would have a murder and on the first day of school to boot!"

"And she's only a teenager!" Holly said nervously. "I'm only 18, it could have been me!"

"If only," Alba sighed and shot Holly an evil look.

"Alba!" Jax admonished. "That's not very nice."

Alba shrugged and crossed her muscular arms across her chest. "I never claimed to be very nice," she whispered under her breath.

"We're supposed to be watching what's going on," Jax insisted. "In case we can help."

"Sorceress Stone said she doesn't need our help," I said shaking my head. She had been perfectly clear there. Anything we might notice, she would surely notice. I looked up and saw her looking at us. She motioned for us to come to her next to the body.

I felt strange nearing the girl's lifeless corpse. I had never seen a dead body in real life before. I mean, I'd seen them on television, but not a real one. "Come on; she wants us," I said. Quietly I ducked my head in reverence to the deceased, and the group of us stepped over the police tape and took a spot next to our teacher. Detective Whitman had gone on to talk to a few of the other officers.

"Ladies," Sorceress Stone said in a hushed voice. "She's been stabbed. Her name is Morgan Hartford. She's 17 years old. She goes to school at St. Michael's the Catholic school up the road. She was last seen by her boyfriend and the school administrative office staff. She had just gotten to school, but then realized she'd forgotten her homework at her house. She lives just a half a mile down the road from the school, that house over there apparently." She pointed to a house just beyond the trees. "It doesn't look like she made it that far."

"Do they have any suspects?" Holly asked, nervously biting her fingernails.

"Not yet, we're going to follow the officers as they do a bit of questioning and maybe ask a few questions ourselves, see if we can get a read on anyone or spark any spirits. But first, we're going to have a look at her. Prepare yourselves; it won't be a pretty sight."

"But…" Sweets began.

"Do we have to?" Jax asked anxiously.

I turned around and bit my lip; I was also hoping that we would get out of that gruesome requirement.

"Why do we have to look at her?" Alba asked pointedly, and suddenly I was thankful that Alba's attitude had come along for the ride.

"Spirits haunt us in a variety of ways. Sometimes they come to us in our dreams. You need to know who we are looking for, don't you?"

Jax looked at the helpless outline of the corpse on the ground. "Couldn't you just show us a picture or something?"

"Oh for goodness sake, if you can't stand and look at a dead body, how can you possibly handle being a witch?" she hissed at us. "There are all sorts of loathsome things that come with being a witch! You must grow a thick skin and a tough stomach."

"Fine," Jax grumbled.

"Detective," the Sorceress called out. "We're ready."

He nodded at her and then motioned to one of his officers who was standing guard next to the body. The officer peeled back the tarp.

I could hear the girls' breaths being sucked in around me. I kept a firm hold of the inside of my lip, to keep from tossing my breakfast onto the crime scene. Somehow I didn't think the Sorceress would look upon that too kindly.

She was a pretty girl with small features and blonde hair. Despite the blue tone to her skin, she looked peaceful. She had a small gold cross hanging around her neck. I silently wondered if she'd fought off her attacker and why had he picked her? Why grab her just to stab her and end her beautiful life? What a sad thing. The energy around me was palpable; everyone was thinking the same things. It could have been any of us.

"Thank you, Officer," Sorceress Stone nodded to the man kindly and then held her hands up to the sky, chanting quietly to herself. I didn't want to open my mouth and risk her wrath to ask her what she was doing.

Finally, she lowered her arms and looked at us. "Let's go girls. We'll start at her school."

We loaded back up into the white van we'd come in, and as we drove away, I noticed a small blonde girl on the side of the road, standing there unnoticed, watching the investigation curiously. She had tiny small features and just as we drove away, I noticed a tiny gold cross hanging around her neck. My blood ran cold. I was sure it was the ghost of Morgan Hartford.

***

St. Michael's was a small Catholic school just up the road. I was surprised that The Sorceress thought all of us witches could just barge right on into a Catholic school, but as we marched in single file, behind Detective Whitman, no one seemed to stop us. "Are the girl's parents here yet?" she asked the detective. He nodded, jerking his head to the side in a quiet suggestion to follow him into the school office where the rest of the people who had last seen her were gathered.

A young man with shaggy brown hair was sobbing on a chair next to the front desk. A teacher was rubbing his back, trying to soothe him. It was obvious that he must be the boyfriend. His anguish was intense, and my heart sank for the boy. I had never been in love before, but his response was what I thought love would do to you if you ever had to say goodbye too soon.

"Sam?" Sorceress asked him.

He looked up at her and then looked to all the rest of us. I was sure we seemed like quite the motley bunch, but he seemed to not even pay us any mind.

"Sam, I'm Miss Stone, we're here to help find out what happened to Morgan. May we ask you a few questions?"

He nodded sadly and ground his eyes with his fists.

She sat down in the chair across from him. "Sam, when was the last time you saw Morgan?" she asked him.

"It was right before 8:00 this morning. The first bell hadn't rung yet, and she realized she'd forgotten her English lit assignment at home on the kitchen table. I told her that I'd just drive her home quick, since she didn't have a car, it would only take a second, but the office said they'd count us both tardy if we weren't back by the first bell. Morgan insisted I go to class; I wouldn't have been eligible for football practice tonight if I got the tardy," he broke down in tears as he choked out the rest of the words. "I should have driven her. I shouldn't have cared about the dumb tardy and about football practice. If I had just driven her, Morgan would still be alive right now."

My heart pumped faster as I listened to his story of regret.

"Now, son, you mustn't blame yourself, you had no idea this would happen," she assured him.

"But Morgan is gone, and it's all my fault," he cried, tears soaked his face.

"Did you do this to her Sam?" she patiently asked him.

He looked up at her, his dark eyes blazed, shocked that she could even ask him such a question. I was equally as shocked that she would straight out ask him. Obviously, he hadn't, the kid was destroyed. "No, I would never do such a horrible thing to Morgan. I *loved* Morgan."

"Then it *isn't* your fault. And you cannot blame yourself for this. Do you understand?" She spoke to him in such a cool, even tone, that I was impressed by her ability to counsel him in such a way.

"Sam, do you have any idea who might have wanted to hurt Morgan?" she asked him.

Sam shook his head. "No, none! Morgan is an amazing girl. Sweet, loving, pure. She would never hurt a fly. I don't understand why someone would want to hurt her!"

"That's what we're trying to figure out, Sam. Did you happen to see anyone follow her out of the building?"

Sam shook his head. "No, when she left, I went to my first class. I thought she'd be back in fifteen minutes. It never occurred to me that she would be in any danger."

"Thank you, Sam, I'm so sorry for your loss." She touched his arm gently. Then quietly, she pushed herself out of the chair and stood, she cocked her head to the side, motioning for us to follow her.

We went into the principal's office where Morgan's parents were inside waiting. Her mother was sobbing on a small settee with a graying man sitting next to her comforting her while another man with his back to us was crying while talking to the detective.

"What are you doing to find my daughter's killer, Detective?" Morgan's father demanded of Detective Whitman.

"Mr. Hartford, we are doing everything we possibly can to get a lead on this case. There was very little evidence at the scene, but I've contacted a local medium to assist. We have had success working with The Institute in the past with cases like these. I think Miss Stone can really help us once again," the Detective said and nodded his head towards our teacher.

The Sorceress stepped forward as we hung quietly just inside the doorway. "I'm Miss Stone, I'm so sorry for your loss Mr. Hartford." Without turning around, he nodded at our teacher, and then covered his face with his hands as another sob racked his body.

"Miss Stone, this is Mary Hartford, Morgan's mother, and this is Oliver Bushwhack, the Guidance Counselor here at the school," Detective Whitman introduced.

Miss Stone nodded, "Mr. Bushwhack, yes, I believe we've met before. Mrs. Hartford, I'm so very sorry for your loss."

As she spoke, Mr. Hartford finally turned around to face us. He was a dark-haired man, with a receding hairline, a bushy black beard, and dark graphite eyes. The hairs on my arms immediately stood on end, and I realized that something about his face looked familiar to me. I searched my memory for a match, but I just couldn't pull it up. It was like it was on the tip of my tongue, but I couldn't spit it out.

"Do you mind if we ask you a few questions?" The Sorceress sat down gently on the other side of Morgan's mother and lightly touched her hand. The small gesture completely changed Mrs. Hartford's body language. Her shoulders, which had seemed tense, loosened up slightly and she seemed very at ease with Miss Stone.

"No, I don't mind," Mrs. Hartford said as she sniffed back tears.

"Mrs. Hartford, did your daughter have any friends

that didn't go to this school?"

She shook her head, "No, Morgan really didn't. Everyone that she hung out with went to St. Michael's. She was on the cheerleading squad here and had lots of friends. She was a member of the tennis team and the youth group, and then she had Sam. Everyone in her world was part of St. Michael's."

"Was there anything unusual about her getting ready for school this morning?" she asked.

Mrs. Hartford thought for a moment before shaking her head. "Nothing," she said splaying her hands out in front of her. "I wish I had seen something, anything to have given me a clue that this was about to happen. I would have prevented it!"

She began sobbing again, and Mr. Bushwhack hugged her lightly. "It might be too soon for some of these questions Miss Stone," he said lightly, looking between the detective and Mr. Hartford. "Morgan was a good girl. This had to be some random act of violence. Everyone here at the school loved her. She was a good student. She had a lot of friends, and she was never in any trouble."

Miss Stone nodded her head. "I see. Well, perhaps we can visit Mr. and Mrs. Hartford another time when things have settled down a bit."

Detective Whitman nodded, and Mr. Bushwhack smiled kindly at Miss Stone.

My spidey senses, however, were tingling like crazy and I was sure it was Mr. Hartford that was setting them off. I could only wonder what it was that I was seeing and not recognizing.

CHAPTER SIX

Even though all I wanted to do was go back to my room and try and figure out where I knew Mr. Hartford's face from and why he was setting off every warning signal in my body – I was too starving to think. The adrenaline rush from the morning's events had bottomed out my blood sugar and left me incredibly famished. I filled my plate in the lunchroom with a heaping pile of fried foods and carb rich delectables and took a seat at one of the marble picnic tables in the courtyard.

The sun was finally out and heating up the September day nicely and yet my heart still hung limply in my chest as I recounted the pain that Morgan's mother and father and boyfriend were feeling right now. It made me incredibly sad to think about, so I tried to focus more on the details of the case than the heartbreak of the family.

Jax followed me to the cafeteria, and as I figured she would, she plopped down next to me with her tray. It seemed that sitting by me wasn't even a question at this point. We were now apparently joined at the hip. I guess a dead body before lunch will do that to ya.

Holly was next to join our table, then Sweets, then finally Alba wandered out of the lunch line and into the courtyard. I wondered if she'd sit with us despite herself. I didn't have to wonder long, when she got within twenty feet of our table, Jax hollered at her. "Hey Alba, over here!"

I rolled my eyes and silently cursed at Jax.

Alba strutted over to our table. "What do you want, Shorty?" she growled.

"Sit with us," Jax begged.

"Whatever," said Alba grudgingly. She dropped her plate on the table with a loud smack, sat her glass of water down next to her plate and then slid in next to Holly. I wondered if she were secretly relieved that she had been invited to join us.

"Can you believe the morning that we've had?" Holly asked as she unwrapped her silverware from its paper napkin holder.

"No kidding, who knew witch college could be so exciting?" Jax added. Her eyes shone with excitement as she plowed into the huge pile of food in front of her.

"Do you guys always eat like that?" Alba asked as she eyed all of our overflowing plates of food.

I choked on my rice as I inhaled the first bite.

"Apparently *you* don't," Alba laughed.

"Aren't you starving? Adrenaline spikes make me hungry!" Sweets said as she began attacking her food with her fork.

Alba shrugged. "Not any more hungry than normal. Haven't you ever heard of the freshman fifteen?"

"That's a myth," I said with my mouth full of a big bite of an egg roll.

"It's not a myth," Holly said sadly. "But that doesn't mean that I'm not starving. I'll watch the figure tomorrow. Today, I need carbs."

"And caffeine," I agreed as I took a huge swallow of the double caramel macchiato that I was excited to have found at the Paranormally Delicious coffee shop next to the Winston Hall cafeteria.

"Ooh, that smells yummy," Sweets cooed. Her face dimpled when she smiled, and something about her really made me actually like her. "Do they have Pumpkin Spice Lattes? They're my favorite!"

"Mine too," Jax agreed.

"Have you tried their Cinnamon Dolce Frappuccinos? Oh, my gosh, they are literally amazing," Holly gushed.

"Are you guys serious right now? You're talking about caffeinated beverages after what we just saw?" cried Alba.

Sweets shook her head seriously and waved a finger in the air. "Oh, no. Pumpkin Spice Lattes don't have caffeine in them."

"Ugh!" Alba growled and slammed both of her palms down on the table on either side of her tray.

We all stopped eating and looked at her.

"What do you want us to say?" I asked her curiously. "I mean, I'm just as upset about the situation as I'm sure the rest of you are, but what are *we* supposed to do?"

Alba shook her head. "I don't know! But we're *witches*. We have *powers*. We should be solving this case and helping that family!"

I looked around the table. Alba's words had shamed the girls we were sitting with and it enraged something deep inside of me. I'd been the victim of shame my entire life. Everyone looked down at their food, except me and Alba. I looked her squarely in the eye. "I *want* to solve this case, Alba. Just like you do. I get that we're witches, but were your powers of telekinesis helping you back there?" I demanded.

When she didn't answer, I continued. "*Yes*, I felt like I was being drawn to her body. Like she wanted us to help her. And *yes,* I felt an energy when I was in the principal's office and felt like I sort of recognized her father, but Morgan's ghost didn't appear to me. Did Morgan's ghost appear to you?"

Alba sat silently for a long moment, and then she looked around the table. The girls had all gotten brave and were staring at her now, challenging her in their own quiet ways. "No," she said quietly and looked down sullenly at her food.

"Alright then. We weren't the ones that died. We still have the ability to enjoy our food. So let's just eat. Maybe something will come to us, and we can help in some way, but for now, all we can do is move forward."

The table went silent after that. We each chewed quietly while lost in our own thoughts. I thought about the fact that I had probably seen Morgan's ghost at the accident sight. I didn't feel too bad for lying to Alba and the rest of the table about seeing Morgan's ghost, because I wasn't 100% sure it was Morgan, plus I truly didn't know what to do with that information. Stone didn't seem to want our help. And really, what would we be able to do on our own? Seeing ghosts had never amounted to anything good back in Illinois, and I certainly had no reason to believe it would help anyone now. If anything, it'd cause waves for me here, and I just wanted to get through the next two years undisturbed.

Two older girls approached us and asked if they could join our table. One had incredibly white hair and the other had hair almost the color of Jax's fake reddish-orange hair. Other than their hair colors they looked identical.

"Hi, I'm Libby," the white haired girl said. "I'm a second year. Girls around here call me the Ice Princess."

Alba looked up at her and laughed as if being called the Ice Princess were silly. "Why do they call you that?" she asked before taking a sip of her water.

Libby shrugged her shoulders and pointed her finger at Alba's glass of water, and it immediately froze solid, encapsulating the tip of Alba's tongue in the glass. "I'm not really sure why they call me that," Libby said, winking at the other girls.

Jax and Holly's eyes widened, and their jaws dropped. "That's really cool," Jax exclaimed.

I couldn't help but giggle at the sight of Alba with her tongue stuck out in front of her, attached to her water glass.

"I'm Cinder, girls call me the Fire Queen," the red haired girl said as she sat down next to Libby. "You wanna know why they call me the Fire Queen?" Cinder asked Alba pointedly.

Alba's eyes widened as she pulled the tip of her tongue out of the glass. She gave a gruff chortle and then shot Cinder a small smile. "Nah, it's alright. I think I'll pass."

"Are you sisters?" I asked. It was a dumb question, even I knew that, but I had to ask it.

"Twins, actually," Cinder said as she took a bite of her hamburger.

"You're *twins*?" Jax asked as if her mind were blown. "That's *so* cool."

"Never seen twins before, Shorty?" Alba asked dryly.

Jax shook her head. "Never seen twin *witches* before."

"Eh, we're a dime a dozen where we come from," Libby admitted.

Sweets' eyes widened. "Where do you come from?"

"Sweden. Our mother is a twin. Her mother was a twin. Our other aunts are twins, our cousins are twins. We will have twins," Libby explained.

Even I was impressed by that.

"Something in the water I guess," Cinder said, dipping a French fry in ketchup.

"Well this is Holly, Alba, Sweets, Mercy, and I'm Jax," Jax pointed to each of us as she introduced us.

"Nice to meet you all, the whole school is buzzing about Sorceress Stone taking you girls to the crime scene today," Libby said, changing the subject.

The thought that that was exciting news to the rest of the school had never occurred to me. I looked around the courtyard and found that almost every set of eyes was on our table.

"What's everyone saying?" Holly asked with interest.

Cinder shrugged. "Just that a girl in town got stabbed and you guys got to go see the body and interview the family and stuff."

I nodded. Well, at least they were getting the rumors right.

"Do any of you think this has anything to do with the Black Witch?" Libby asked with a conspiratory look and a hushed voice.

All of us new girls looked at each other curiously.

"The Black Witch?" Sweets asked, her voice catching nervously in her throat. "There's a Black Witch?"

"You girls don't know about the Black Witch?" Libby lowered herself to practically lay out on the table.

Holly shook her head. "I don't think any of us do."

"The Black Witch lives high up on the hill. Have you ever noticed the turret in the distance?"

Holly and Alba both nodded. "We can see it from our room," Holly said.

"She's a disaster. She's completely evil. I've personally never met her, but the stories about her are crazy. Her face has been burned by acid. She's horrible to look at and so she never comes out of hiding, and if anyone goes to her, she eats them," Libby shared.

"She eats them?" I asked skeptically. I hardly believed that for a second.

"You don't know that Lib," Cinder pointed out. "We shouldn't spread rumors like that."

"Well, that's what *everyone* says," her sister pouted.

"Why would The Black Witch kill Morgan?" Alba asked Libby.

"I didn't say she killed her. I just asked if anyone is suspecting her. I mean, she'd be the first person that *I'd* suspect."

"Why would you suspect her?" I asked pointedly. "You just said that she never leaves her house."

Libby shrugged. "She might leave *sometimes*. I mean, wouldn't she have to get, like, groceries or something?"

I rolled my eyes.

Sweets shook her head emphatically. "No, no, not necessarily. A lot of grocery stores have online ordering now and will deliver right to your door."

"You guys, I'm sure this Black Witch has nothing to do with Morgan's death," I discounted the notion as ridiculous.

"You don't know that Mercy," Holly said, biting her fingernails once again.

"No, I got the distinct feeling it was a man that did this," I said. I knew my gut was leading me in that direction, but I just didn't understand why. But my mother always told me to follow my gut, even though usually, it only led me to the kitchen.

"I got that feeling too," Alba agreed.

"Well, maybe it was someone from the wizard school," Cinder suggested and tilted her head towards the wizard's side of The Institute.

I nodded. That thought really hadn't occurred to me, but now that Cinder said it, I had to give that some serious consideration. I didn't know anything about the guys. In fact, I hadn't even met any of them yet. Granted I had only been on campus a total of 24 hours, but one would think we would have seen the men during breakfast at the very least, but none had appeared.

"Where are the men anyway? Don't we share the courtyard?" I asked.

Cinder nodded her head. "We do. They try and keep our class schedules so that the men eat their meals at alternate times than the women. I think it's just because there's not a ton of seating out here, so they try and stagger it so we don't all fight for space to sit outside. Occasionally you'll see one of the guys who missed breakfast join the girls or vice versa. Usually the only time we interact with the Wiz Kids is on the weekends."

Alba harrumphed loudly. "You call the men Wiz Kids? I bet they *love* that."

Cinder shot Alba an annoyed glance.

"What happens on the weekends?" Holly asked. Her interest had been piqued.

"We have social hours and sometimes dances or other events. It's not that they try and keep us apart or anything, they just really have two separate schools with a common area in between."

"So, you think the wizards could have something to do with this?"

Cinder met my eyes seriously. "Around here, you have to consider *everyone* a suspect."

57

"Why is that?"

"There is so much magical energy circulating through these buildings and through this town. Aspen Falls isn't just your usual, run of the mill town, you know. Witches and Wizards have been coming to this school for centuries. The town is used to us. Libby could literally go downtown right now and shoot the waterfall in the center of town. Freeze it solid. Not a single townsperson would blink an eye."

"You're kidding me?" I couldn't believe it. I'd never been in a place that accepted witches like that. It seemed like a fairy tale to me.

"Not even remotely," Libby agreed. "I mean think about it. They have a college called the Paranormal Institute. People come from all over to go to this school. Some of *the* biggest names in Witchcraft and Wizardry have gone to school here."

"Morticia Addams went to school here," said Cinder with a convincing nod.

Jax laughed. "She did not, that's a lie."

Libby shook her head. "No, it's not. She went to school here. So did the Long Island Medium. What was her name?" Libby asked her sister.

"Theresa Caputo."

"Yeah, Theresa Caputo, she went to school here."

I let my head fall into my hands. These girls were a bunch of nuts.

Jax rolled her eyes and sat up straighter. "Now I know you two are full of it. I've never seen anything on the school's website about having famous people having gone to school here. They'd advertise the heck out of that if it were true."

Cinder shrugged. "Would they? That would draw attention to the school. There are a lot of witch hunters in the world. Why would the school want to draw big amounts of publicity? Witches know how to find the school if they need to. That's really all that matters."

"We're losing track of the point here," I finally said. I'd had enough of Libby and Cinder's silly stories. "The point you were trying to make is that you think we should consider everyone a suspect."

"Oh, yes," Cinder said, nodding her head as if she'd just remembered what she was talking about. "Everyone is a suspect. You have no idea how many retired witches and wizards are living in Aspen Falls. I know for a fact that the town baker is a potion-maker."

Sweets' eyes opened wide. "Really? What kind of potions?"

Cinder shrugged, "Just your basic herbal remedies for back pain, joint pain, high blood pressure – you know, baked with love in a loaf of bread."

"Oooh, maybe I should go meet the baker someday. I'd love to do an internship down there."

Alba leaned forward and looked across the table at me. Her eyes met mine, and I felt like she was trying to tell me something without actually telling me something. I raised one eyebrow and tipped my head curiously to the side. Why would *Alba* be trying to tell me something? When I didn't get the message from her eyes, she reluctantly whispered across the table. "Mercy, may I have a word with you?"

It was a small table, her whisper carried across it, and everyone stopped eating and looked at me. My eyes swiveled from side to side watching the girls' curious expressions.

When I didn't budge from the table, Alba added, "In private, please?" She stood up and took her half eaten plate of food and glass of water with her.

I looked down at my beautiful fried delectables sadly. I grabbed another egg roll and my Paranormally Delicious coffee cup and stood up, following her back into our building. She didn't stop when inside but continued up the stairs where she halted in front of my dorm room door.

"Can we talk in here?" she asked me. I thought I detected a hint of impatience, but pushed that idea out of my head immediately.

"Sure?" I said curiously. I pulled my lanyard out of my sweatshirt and unlocked my door, letting us both in the room. I sat my coffee cup down on my desk and flopped down on the bottom bunk. "Have a seat," I offered and gestured towards a chair.

She sat. Her movements were jerky and unnatural, and I could immediately tell that she had something important to talk to me about. My heart jerked up into my throat as I sat up.

Alba leaned forward and met my eyes. I braced myself for the words to follow. "I know you saw Morgan's ghost at the crime scene."

CHAPTER SEVEN

"What did you just say?" I asked, stunned. Heat immediately began filling my cheeks. How in the world did she know that?

"You heard me, Red," she answered, blatantly rolling her eyes at me.

Alba's attitude hit me like a bag of bricks to the face; my walls immediately went flying up. "I'm sorry, *why* would you think that?" I asked, unwilling to admit anything to her.

"Because on very rare occasion I have the ability to read minds," she reminded me.

Ugh, I groaned to myself. I had forgotten about that.

"What I don't understand is why you would keep that information to yourself?" she demanded. "In fact, you *lied* to us about it."

I crossed my arms defensively and felt myself growing angry. "Why would I tell *you* anything? You don't even *like* me."

"I don't *dislike* you," she said flippantly.

"So you're saying you *like* me." I clarified.

"Don't flatter yourself. I'm only asking because the rest of those idiots don't have a brain to split between them and I thought you could use a little help finding her ghost."

"So you're saying I have a brain to split? Gee thanks, you want half?" I deflected with a laugh.

Alba sighed and sat back in her chair. "I'm trying to be serious here. I know you saw Morgan's ghost."

My mind reeled. I didn't know what to say. I sat there quiet for a moment, trying to gather my thoughts when all of a sudden, a big black cat jumped onto the window sill of my second-floor dorm room. I looked at it curiously. How in the world had he just done that? I stood up and immediately looked out the window; there was a fire escape balcony just next to us. He must have jumped over from there.

"Hi little guy," I said kindly as he jumped through my open window and into my room. "You can't be in here buddy."

"Your cat?" Alba asked me with narrowed eyes. "I didn't think we were allowed to have pets."

I shrugged. "Not mine." I plucked him up off the floor and sat back down on my bed with him, petting his back mindlessly. "I'll take him outside in a minute."

"We need to talk about this, Red. I know you saw Morgan. Why didn't you share that information when we were there?"

I took a deep breath and then sighed, slumping down into my chair. "I didn't know what to do. Stone was extremely to the point when she said she didn't want any of our help. Besides, I'm not 100% sure it was her."

"Where did you see her?"

"On the side of the road, it was like she was watching the whole scene go down from afar. She looked scared." As I finally had a moment to think of Morgan, my heart fell for the poor girl.

"Of course she looked scared. Wouldn't *you* be scared if you were watching your murder investigation scene play out right in front of your eyes? You should have said something. Now she's probably scared and alone."

I looked down at the floor regretfully. I could tell she felt bad about that. "I just thought Miss Stone would handle things, and then she didn't."

"Maybe she didn't see her," Alba suggested.

"Well, duh, Captain Obvious," I said sarcastically. "Of course she didn't see her. If she had seen her, we'd have this murder solved by now."

"You don't know that. Some ghosts don't know who killed them."

"I know that. But a lot of them do know," I argued.

She stood up and put her hands on her hips. "We've got to do something. I can't handle going about my day now with Morgan's ghost wandering Aspen Falls. What if she falls into the hands of the wrong person? Cinder said that there are other witches and wizards running around the town. We're not all *good* witches you know."

"Yeah," I said, eyeing Alba keenly. "I know this."

"Oh quit. Just because I'm gruff doesn't mean I'm not a good witch. I'm a good witch. I'm just not a *nice* witch."

"Umm, so does that make you a *bitchy witch?*" I asked with a snicker.

Alba rolled her eyes at me. "We're going to need a car if we're going back down there. I don't have one here, do you?"

I shook my head. "Nope, Mom drove mine back to Illinois."

"Ugh, we're going to have to involve the other girls then. One of them has to have driven here."

"Sweets has a car, I saw her unloading it on the first day of class," I remembered immediately.

"Ok, we'll get Sweets to take us, but we are *not* taking tweedle dee and tweedle dum," Alba insisted as she opened my door.

I scooped up the cat and followed Alba out the door, along the hall, and down the stairs. In the courtyard, I sat the cat down, patted his head and gave his rear an encouraging little shove when he didn't just run off right away. "Go on, go," I said to him. He was such a pretty cat. I almost wished I could keep him; after all didn't every good witch need a black cat to keep her company?

Sweets was still sitting at the table with Holly and Jax. Libby and Cinder had gone. Alba and I looked at each other, unsure of how to talk to Sweets about using her car without Holly and Jax overhearing.

I jerked my head towards Sweets as if to tell Alba to

get moving. She cleared her throat. "Sweets, can we have a talk with you?" Alba called in her sweetest voice.

Sweets' face lit up. She practically leaped out of her seat racing to get next to us and be in on whatever we were cooking up. "What's up girls?"

I looked back at the table. Jax and Holly were leaning back, straining to overhear our conversation, 'accidentally.' "We need to borrow your car."

"My – car? Why?" she asked, surprised at the request.

I shrugged. I didn't know if I should tell her that I had seen Morgan's ghost.

"Red saw Morgan's ghost down at the crime scene," Alba admitted quickly.

I guess we weren't planning to keep that a secret.

Sweets smiled excitedly, and her eyes widened. "Oh, and you want me to drive you?"

Immediately Holly and Jax shot out of their seats. "Where ya driving them, Sweets? Can we go too?" Jax asked excitedly.

"I'll just go grab my purse," Holly squealed, bouncing on her toes, making her breasts jiggle visibly in her low cut blouse. "This is *so* fun. It's like we're detectives!"

Alba rolled her eyes. "No, we can't all go."

"Why does Sweets get to go?" Holly demanded to know.

"Because she brought her car to college," I pointed out. "And we need a ride."

Jax stuck her lip out. "So? Why do you get to go?"

"Because … Alba wants me to go," I said, unsure if that was a good reason.

"Where does Alba want you to go?" Holly asked.

"Back to the crime scene," Sweets announced.

Holly and Jax's heads swiveled immediately to Alba. "Why do you want to go back to the crime scene?"

Alba groaned. I knew that was exactly what she was trying to avoid, but it was too late. Now they'd all have to go. "Ugh, Mercy saw Morgan."

"We all saw Morgan," Holly said in confusion.

"I saw her *ghost*."

"Ohhh," Jax and Holly cooed in unison.

"We're going," Jax said sternly. "Holly go get your purse. Sweets, get the car."

I looked at Jax with surprise. Suddenly she was in charge of the situation?

Sweets made a face. "Guys, what about classes? We can't just skip our afternoon classes on the first day of school."

I looked at the plastic Batman watch on my wrist. "Next class isn't until 1:30; we can make it there and back in time if we hustle. Holly, leave the purse, you won't need it. Come on, let's go."

The crime scene wasn't very far away. Before we knew it, we were cruising down the tree lined road and hoping that Morgan's ghost would still be there. We pulled up to the scene and were disappointed to find out that the body had already been moved and there were no cop cars to be seen. Traffic was moving as usual in the area. We pulled over to the side of the road.

"You girls stay in here," I ordered. "Come on Alba, let's go look around."

Alba and I got out of the car. She waltzed over to the blood stain on the side of the asphalt and closed her eyes, with her arms extended and her palms facing the sky, she began to meditate as Stone had done earlier. I watched her only briefly but then felt the flesh on my arms begin to prickle.

"See anything?" Holly asked from inside the car.

I held a finger to my lips to silence her and let my senses take over. They got stronger as I walked towards Alba and they played the hot/cold game with me until I was standing just beside the road. I looked around me, fully expecting to see Morgan's ghost, but saw nothing. Finally, I looked down at my feet. A small piece of asphalt had dislodged itself from the road, I squatted down and lifted it up and flipped it over, examining it closely. Nothing exciting jumped out at me. I lowered my arm to set it back down. But before I did, I noticed a shiny object hidden underneath it. I picked it up, and my body got the chills. It was a small golden ring with a little cross on it with a tiny gemstone flake set inside of it. I could see a little inscription inside. I rolled it around in my fingers and then looked at it more closely. The inscription read *True Love Waits*.

Immediately, I knew it had to be Morgan's. I stood up quickly and brought it to the car.

"Check this out," I said and showed them the ring.

Jax took it from me. "I've seen these before. It's a purity ring."

"A purity ring? Meaning she was saving herself for marriage?" Holly asked Jax.

Jax nodded. "If it was hers, then yeah, I think that's what that means."

I handed the ring to Holly. "See if you get a read on this, Holly."

Holly looked at the ring and then looked at me like I was crazy. "I told you guys, I can't summon it. Sometimes it works and sometimes it doesn't."

I shrugged and leaned up against the car door. "No harm in trying, right? If it was Morgan's maybe it will give us some information."

Holly took the ring and closed her eyes, trying to summon the energy from the ring. I looked at Alba; she was still standing there, chanting quietly. I was suddenly thankful that there were no cars passing us by, they'd think we were a bunch of weirdoes if they had.

Finally, Holly opened her eyes. "Nope, nada," she said and handed the ring back to me.

"It's ok. We'll give the ring to the cops. It might not have even been hers," I admitted, though my senses were telling me it was hers. "Alba, she's not here. Let's go," I hollered as I got back into the front seat of the car.

Alba opened one eye and looked at the car. She closed it again and chanted one last time. Finally, she threw her hands down to her sides. They hit her thighs with a loud clap, and her body slumped over in defeat. She came back to the car and got in the back next to Holly. "Let's go Sweets," she sighed.

"Don't worry about it, Alba. We tried," I told her.

"Yeah, we tried! The body isn't here anymore, her ghost is probably with her body," Holly said nonchalantly.

Alba's eyes perked up. "Duh, she's with her body! Sweets, we need to find the Aspen Falls morgue. Anyone know this town at all?"

Jax nodded her head. "Yeah, I know where it is. Can you make a U-turn here Sweets?"

CHAPTER EIGHT

The Aspen Falls Medical Center was quiet when we arrived. The trees over the slumbering brick building swayed in the breeze as the five of us exited Sweets' four-door Ford Taurus.

"How are we doing this?" I asked as we all approached the front door looking like a pirate band of misfits.

Everyone looked at me curiously.

"We can't just go in there and ask to see Morgan Hartford's body!" I pointed out.

Alba nodded. "She's right. We're going to have to be subtle about it. Let me do the talking."

She opened the door, and the five of us quietly filed in behind her. We followed the signs through the brightly lit sterile hallways to the double glass doors which read Aspen Falls Morgue. A young man in a white lab coat was working on the computer at the front counter. He was in his mid-twenties with sandy blonde hair, broad muscular shoulders and a tattoo of a bird and a cross on his forearm. Alba approached him, and the man looked up. His eyes moved from Alba to me to Jax to Sweets and then settled on Holly. A slow smile spread across his face as he noticed her low cut blouse and swollen exposed breasts.

I laughed to myself. I was right. Holly had the power of enchantment! Alba opened her mouth to speak, but before she could, I grabbed her arm and pulled her back towards me and then put my flattened palm into the small of Holly's back and shoved her forward.

"Excuse me, sir, we are doing a paper on morgues for college, and we have to ask some questions, do you have a minute for Holly here to ask you a couple of questions?" I asked.

His eyes lit up as Holly approached him. I winked at her as she looked back at me and immediately she knew what to do. "Hi, I'm Holly," she purred sweetly, leaning over the counter towards him, allowing him access to the full range of her physical attributes. "I just have a few questions; it really should only take a few minutes." She batted her long fake eyelashes at him and smiled sweetly.

He nodded excitedly. I was sure nothing in his day had compared to having Holly's undivided attention for a few minutes. "Yeah, absolutely. What do you need to know?" he asked her.

"Oh, you know, umm, where do you put your bodies?" Holly asked awkwardly. I wanted to palm my forehead. We were going to have to work on Holly's extemporaneous abilities if she were going to play detective again.

He pointed towards the swinging door off to the side of him. "There's a system back there. I can give you a tour if you like?" he offered.

I shook my head vigorously at Holly hoping she'd get the hint. We couldn't very well snoop around for ghosts with him leading the way.

"Oh, no, no need for a tour," she cooed brightly.

I stepped forward. "Excuse me, sir. Do you have a restroom?"

He barely acknowledged me as he pointed to the same swinging door he'd just offered to show us. "Through those doors, first door on your left."

"Great, thanks. Anyone else need to use the restroom?" I asked the girls.

Alba, Jax, and Sweets raised their hands in unison. "Holly, we all have to go, can you handle the interview by yourself?"

Holly cleared her throat nervously. I could tell she was upset with me for leaving her to deal with the attendant alone, but we needed to look for Morgan. "Umm, sure. Yeah, totally. I'll be fine."

We didn't wait around for him to change his mind about allowing us to use the restroom. Instead, we slid through the swinging door and past the restroom and went directly to the end of the hallway. I peered through the little glass window and saw the lockers body coolers lining the walls. "This way," I whispered nervously, suddenly scared that we would be caught before we could find Morgan's ghost.

The four of us slid into the large open room. It was sterile and cold with stainless steel doors on the walls. Each had a little tag on it, indicating who was inside.

"Shouldn't Morgan's ghost just be hanging out around here? Do we really have to go opening drawers to find her ghost?" Sweets asked apprehensively.

Alba nodded her head. "Yeah, see anything Red? It's not like she's going to be lying inside the drawer."

I looked around unhappily. "Nothing."

Morgan Hartford's name was printed carefully on a little tag on one of the coolers. "Here she is. We're going to have to open it. Her ghost could be in there with her," I finally said. I wasn't looking forward to seeing Morgan's lifeless body again, but we all knew it needed to be done.

Alba nodded.

Sweets looked away as I pulled open the stainless steel door and pulled out the drawer.

My jaw dropped as it slid out of the chamber. Not only was there no ghost in the drawer, but there was also no body.

"Where is she?" Jax asked immediately.

"They've got to have her somewhere else. Maybe they are doing an autopsy!" suggested Alba.

"Or maybe she's in one of the other drawers. Should we open them all?" Sweets proposed.

I shook my head vehemently. I was not about to look at any more dead bodies today. "No way they'd put her dead body in a different drawer. She just got here!"

"She's got to be in an examination room

somewhere," Alba said. "Let's go look in the other rooms."

We slipped out of the locker room area and up the hallway. There were only four more doors, one of which was the bathroom. We peeked in the other three and were frustrated to discover that Morgan's body wasn't in any of those rooms either. Finally, we made our way back to the front counter.

Holly appeared much more relaxed when we found her again. "Hi girls," she chirped cheerfully. "Alex and I were just talking, and you know ... there's a big street dance Saturday night."

"Is that right?" I asked, not in the least bit interested.

"Yes, it's the town's annual Autumnal Equinox celebration. Everyone comes out to celebrate. He asked if I'd like to go with him!" Holly said excitedly.

I looked at Alex. He beamed with pride at having such a hot date for the dance. I assumed he had no idea that he had just asked a witch out for dinner and dancing. But then again, considering that the town was used to us paranormal beings, perhaps he'd asked a witch out before.

"Well, how nice," I drawled. "Listen, Alex, do you have anywhere else that you keep your dead bodies? Like perhaps if they are undergoing an autopsy?"

Alex shook his head. "Autopsy's are performed on site. If one needs to be done on a body, we have a room in the back that we do it in."

"In the back of *this* office?" I clarified.

He nodded. "Yup, the room next to the bathroom

you just used."

The girls and I looked at each other.

"If someone was killed, in say a murder, would their body come directly here from the crime scene?" Alba asked him. "Or would the police keep it for some reason."

I thought for sure he'd be onto us with that question.

"Yes, as a matter of fact, they come directly here. We actually just had that happen today, funny you should ask. A girl in town was killed, and the police brought her body here where she will stay until the funeral home comes to get her," he explained patiently.

Jax, Alba, Sweets and I all nodded our heads and smiled. That was where Morgan must have gone. "Oh, I see. So the funeral home probably came to get her already."

Alex furrowed his eyebrows together. "The new girl? Oh, no. She just got here. She'll be here for awhile before the funeral home guys come to get her."

"Is it possible the funeral home guys came to get her while you were out to lunch?" I asked nervously.

He shook his head. "No. I ate lunch at my desk. I have hardly moved since she got here. Besides, they have to check her out and here's my list. See," he said, showing us the clipboard. "She's still here. We have to be very systematic about all of that."

Alba set her dark eyes intently on Alex. "Then where is Morgan?" she asked him.

He regarded Alba and the rest of us skeptically. "I didn't say her name. How did you know her name?"

"It doesn't matter," Alba told him firmly. "She's not here. Where is she?"

Alex stood up. He was finally starting to get the idea that we were working on more than a school report. He grabbed the phone receiver from the landline in front of him. "You went back there? What's going on? I'm going to have to call security. You girls shouldn't have gone back there."

I rolled my eyes at him. "You let us go back there."

"I let you use the restroom. I didn't say you could go in the other rooms!" He argued as he began to dial a number.

Alba pushed the button down on the phone to kill the dial tone. "You don't need to call anyone. We just want to know where Morgan's body is."

"She's back there. I locked her away myself thirty minutes ago."

Alba shook her head. "Hate to break it to you Al, but Morgan ain't back there."

"She is too," he disagreed.

"She's not," I agreed with Alba. "We just looked. She's not in the drawer."

Alex looked at each of us nervously. "What's going on here?"

"You don't want to know," Holly assured him.

"You're in on this?" he accused suddenly.

Holly's eyes widened, and she looked at Alex nervously. "Well, no, I, uh…" She looked at the four of us; hoping one of us would come to her rescue.

"Ugh! Figures!" he complained, stomping his foot on

the ground.

"Does this mean our date for the dance is off?" she whined.

He rolled his eyes at her. "You girls don't know what you're talking about. I'll go back there and prove it to you. Morgan is there."

We followed Alex to the locker room and quickly proved to him that she wasn't in her drawer. He looked at us through narrowed eyes. "What have you girls done with her body?"

"Ugh!" I hollered indignantly. "We just got here! What have *you* done with her body?"

"I didn't do anything! I put her where she belonged, ate my lunch, and then you five show up and things went haywire! I bet you're all a bunch of those paranormals from The Institute, aren't you?"

We all exchanged nervous glances, but no one fessed up.

"Yeah, I knew it. What did you do? Use a magic spell to make her body float away?"

Holly laughed. "Oh, Alex, hardly! That's not how magic works. It isn't, right girls?"

I shrugged. "I have no idea how her body disappeared."

"Yeah, me either," Alba agreed. "But if he put her in there thirty minutes ago and now she's gone, there's a good chance magic is to blame here. But it wasn't our magic," she assured him, putting her hands up in front of her.

"Alex, we didn't do it, swear," Holly said, her blue

eyes twinkled in the light. "We got called down to the crime scene earlier to investigate. We wanted to see the body one more time, and that's why we're here."

"I'm not sure I can believe that," he said shaking his head.

Alba shrugged. "Call Detective Whitman then. He'll tell you. In fact, we need to call him now anyway. You've got a problem – Morgan's body is missing, and we need to get it back!"

***

Detective Whitman was not a happy camper when he discovered that Alex had allowed the body to be stolen and that we were on the scene to discover it. "Why are you girls involved?" he asked, waving us away like a swarm of pesky mosquitoes. "I was sure that Miss Stone asked you to let her handle things."

"We thought we sensed something, so we went back to the scene of the crime to see if the energy returned," I explained to him trepidatiously.

He nodded. "I see. And did it?"

"In a way – we found this," I told him and pulled the small ring out of my pocket. "We think it was Morgan's."

He looked down at the ring and a little smile spread across his face. "It is hers. Her father told me that her ring was missing. He said she'd gotten it from the youth group at her church. It's a purity ring. He'll be glad to get it back. Where did you find it? I had officers combing the whole area!"

"It was under a piece of asphalt. Like it slipped off of her finger during a struggle. I bet it got kicked under the rock." Sharing my suspicions made me feel better, and I felt myself begin to relax for a moment.

"Alright, so you found a piece of evidence, that still doesn't excuse the fact that Morgan's body is now missing!" he argued, his mustache twitched as he looked the five of us over. "You know I'm going to have to report this incident to Miss Stone for investigation at The Institute."

My heart stopped for a moment. My mother would *kill* me if she knew I was already skipping classes in college. Not only that, but if it got back to the Dubbsburg Police Department that I was involved in the case of a missing body, they'd no doubt revoke the plea bargain that I do a two-year stint at The Institute instead of a year's stint in the Dubbsburg County correctional facility. I shook my head. "Aww, do you have to tell Miss Stone. It's our first day. We were only trying to help," I asked sweetly, giving him the best sad face I could muster without making myself sick.

"Yes, I have to tell Miss Stone. She can't have her students going off the rails on the first day! Now, the five of you need to get back to The Institute before I arrest you for impeding an investigation!"

"Fine, do what you gotta do, we were just trying to help that girl's family," I growled and then waved the girls towards me. "Let's go girls."

One by one we each spun on our heels and walked

away, snubbing our noses at the Detective as we passed him.

Sorceress Stone was waiting for us when we got back. No sooner had we stepped foot onto the oversized tile floor in Winston Hall, than we were pounced on by her highness herself.

"What did I tell you girls?" she immediately fumed, summoning up a swirling storm of energy around us. My hair began to get sucked up into the vortex of her heated emotions.

I closed my eyes and counted to ten, trying to calm my own emotional thunderstorm bubbling up inside of me. We were only trying to help. And now we would be punished for our actions.

Sweets immediately apologized. "I'm sorry Sorceress Stone. We were only trying to help."

"Silence!" she hollered. "I was extremely specific when I told you that I would handle things. You were to be eyes and ears only. You were not to speak!"

"We didn't speak," I argued. "When we were down at the crime scene, we didn't do anything wrong. We went back because an energy was pulling us back."

Sorceress Stone shot me an evil glare, and I suddenly wondered if she were The Black Witch that the Fire & Ice twins had been referring to. "Your old school warned me about you, this was your doing, wasn't it?"

I stepped forward, as I felt a rod of steel shoot down my spine. I was not about to take any guff from this lady, even if it did mean I had to go to a correctional facility for the next year. It was better than being demonized by this crazy witch. I was just about to tell her where she could stick her little air show when Alba put one arm in front of me and stepped forward.

"It wasn't Mercy. It was me. I insisted she go with me back down to the crime scene and I asked the girls to all go with me," Alba bravely admitted with her own stiff posture.

I looked at Alba. I couldn't believe she wouldn't just let me take the blame for everything. "It was both of us," I said, stepping forward, shoulder to shoulder with her.

Holly stepped forward next, then Jax, then Sweets. "We all did it."

"I know you all did it. I saw you walk in together! Detective Whitman told me you were all down there. What? You think this show of solidarity will do something to my heart? This isn't about my heart, ladies. This is about a serious police investigation. It's not a game. You are *not* to get involved in this case. One more misstep like this and I'll lock you all away in the highest room of this school! Do you understand?"

Sweets immediately nodded. "Yes, ma'am."

Jax and Holly nodded, and Jax linked arms with me. I could tell she wanted me to agree too.

"I understand," I finally said in a huff.

"Fine," Alba said angrily.

"Now go to your rooms, I've had enough of looking at the five of you for one day!"

CHAPTER NINE

"This sucks," Alba said. Lying on her back atop the furry rug in my dorm room she tossed a beanbag up and down. I couldn't help but agree with her. This did suck, and the pure deliciousness of the Baked Apple Pie candle flickering near the open window didn't make it suck any less.

"I can't believe we've been here all of a day and we're already in trouble!" Holly complained. "I hope this doesn't affect us getting to do the social this Friday night."

Sweets looked at her curiously. "There's a social this Friday night? With the boys?"

"Yeah, with the boys," I said with a little laugh. "Who'd you think? With the teachers?"

Sweets smiled timidly. "Oh, yeah, of course. Boys sort of make me nervous."

I sat up straight in my chair and peered at Sweets

curiously. "But you're a matchmaker. How can boys make you nervous? You put couples together, right?"

Sweets nodded. "Yeah, I've put *other* couples together, but I can't do a spell on myself! I've never had a boyfriend."

I sighed and slumped back against the hard dresser drawers I was sitting next to. It was hard to have a boyfriend when you were a witch. No one ever wanted to date the witch. People always had something jack-assy to say, 'Don't date her! She's a witch. Witches are worse than Taylor Swift, they won't just write a song about you when you break up, they will put a hex on you!'

Yes, dating in the witch world as a teenager was non-existent. My mother told me it would get better as an adult. She said being a witch was sort of an aphrodisiac to men in their late 20's and early 30's. Unfortunately, she had added, it was mostly more of a sexual fetish for those men, and they weren't always one to stick around for the long haul.

Case in point, my father. He had been the hit it and quit it type of guy, and while I'd always envisioned meeting him someday, my mom told me I wouldn't like him. He was too handsome for his own good, he was cocky and quite the ladies man. "*Who wants a guy like that for a father?*" she would always ask me. This always made me feel bad, I mean, I didn't have a choice in the matter. Not only hadn't I gotten to *pick* my father, but I also hadn't gotten to *meet* my father either.

"It's ok, Sweets. I've never had a real boyfriend either," I admitted.

Sweets stopped licking the frosting off of the cupcake she was holding and looked at me in surprise. "But you're so beautiful!"

I gave her a little smirk, "Thanks, Sweets. You're beautiful too. Beauty's got nothing to do with it though. Boys like *normal* girls. Boys don't like girls like us."

"Girls like what?" Holly demanded. Her ice blue eyes glinted in the sunlight. Apparently,   she took offense to being lumped in with the rest of us undateable witches.

"Relax, Cosmo, don't get your tights in a twist," I said. "You're a witch just like the rest of us."

"Cosmo?" Jax asked.

"Yeah, Miss Cosmopolitan over there. She's got the perfect platinum blonde hair, the perfect blue eyes, and the perfect, flawless skin. She's got the boobs, the butt, the perfect waistline; she's like a dream come true for a guy. Apparently, she doesn't want to be lumped in with us undateable witches."

Holly shook her head excitedly, "You're looking at this all wrong Mercy. We aren't undateable witches! I never had a problem dating in high school."

"Of course not! That's my point! Look at you!"

"Yes, look at me! I take pride in my appearance. Call me Cosmo or tell me I'm vain, but the fact of the matter is, I have never let being a witch stand in the way of me meeting boys."

"Not everyone can look like you, Cosmo. The rest of us are just plain looking girls that are witches. You're the exception, not the rule!" I argued.

Holly shrugged and sat back down. "All I'm saying is

some of you could try a little harder."

Alba caught her beanbag in mid-air and then let a big chortle escape her lips. "Ohhh, snap."

"You think you're not included in that slight?" I said sideways to Alba.

Jax put her hands on her hips and bounced up off the bed. "Well, I know I certainly try hard," she pouted.

"Jax, you try *too* hard. What are you trying to prove anyway?" Holly asked her pointedly.

"Ohhh," I hollered, letting my hand cover my broad smile.

Jax looked hurt. "I'm not trying to *prove* anything. What do you mean?"

"I mean, you look like a *witch*!" Holly spat distastefully.

Jax furrowed her eyebrows and made a face. "Isn't that the point?"

"No!" I laughed, "That's *not the point!* You're at *witch* school. We're *all* witches. Why do you need to dress like you're an actress at a Renaissance Festival or something?"

"I like dressing this way," she countered. "It's cute."

"I think she looks adorable," Sweets added, agreeing with Jax.

"You would," Holly said, rolling her eyes.

"What's that supposed to mean?" Sweets demanded.

"That dress – you look like your grandmother dressed you – from her dead friend's rummage sale," Holly admitted.

Appalled Sweets looked down at the sunflower-covered sundress she wore. "You don't like my dress?"

"It certainly isn't flattering," Holly said flippantly, lifting her left shoulder in a *'just saying'* sort of way.

"It's not?" Sweets' bottom lip began to quiver.

"That's enough Holly," I finally said. I should have ended this awhile ago.

"What? I'm just saying, girl has got some boobs and ass. Why not flaunt it? Why hide it all away in a field of daisies?"

"They're sunflowers," Sweets whispered under her breath.

"Her dress certainly doesn't show off the goods to boys. When you're overcoming the odds, like we are, you've got to advertise the merchandise a little, ladies." With that she readjusted her breasts inside of her shirt, hoisting them higher, until they threatened a wardrobe malfunction. "Hidden away in a ratty old hoodie, these puppies aren't going to sell themselves!"

"False advertising is illegal, ya know," I quipped. I knew Holly's last comment was for me and my non-descript style. I'd never been the girly girl, the fashion girl, the makeup girl. I was a witch – and a bit of a tomboy, and lately, I'd led with that. It was just easier. Who wanted to allow someone to get to know you, you let your walls down, let them in, and then the minute your secret is revealed – bam! – they're out the door so fast it knocks the broomstick off the mantel. That didn't make any sense to me.

Alba laughed again. "Ohhh!"

Holly shot me an evil look. "These aren't fake, just so you know. I grow all my own produce."

"Sure ya do. They didn't come free with seven pairs of panties at the mall, did they?"

The blonde crossed her arms over her chest, "No! And even if they did, what's so wrong with that? You guys! We're witches. It's an obstacle, not a road block. We're still *women*. We're not freaking *corpses*. And I think you want to start the social night on the right foot. If this is the first time we're going to meet some of the men around here we need to put our best selves out there. They're like us. They aren't like guys from back home. These guys are going to be paranormal also. Witches aren't going to scare them away."

I hadn't thought of it like that before. Everyone here was like me. *Everyone.* "We got it, Cosmo."

Sweets shot Holly a shy look. "I only brought dresses to wear. My mother said they look cute on me."

"There's got to be a fairy godmother around this town somewhere!" Holly suggested with a smirk.

Alba, who had been taking in the whole conversation rather quietly, finally sat up. "Fairy godmothers and men aren't going to solve all of our problems."

"Yeah," I agreed and fell back onto my bed with a heavy heart. "What do we do now?"

Just then I heard a familiar thud outside my dorm room window.

"Hey fella," Jax cooed. "How'd you get up here?"

I turned my head to the side and saw Jax pulling a big black cat out of the window and into our room. I sat up in surprise. "He's back?"

"You know him?" Jax asked me with surprise.

I shook my head. "No. Do you?"

She shook her head also. "Nope. Never seen him before."

"He was in here earlier today, I feel like someone brought their cat to college and he keeps escaping from their dorm room."

"We could put up a sign?" Sweets suggested.

"Nah, Stone won't let us have pets," Alba countered. "That'd only be stirring the pot around here."

"So what do we do with him?" Holly asked.

"I'll take him back outside again. He'll get the hint," I said, pulling him into my arms and stroking his soft black fur. "But for now, he can chill here with us. Can't you little guy?" I scratched under his chin and he rubbed his long body up against mine in a friendly manner. I could tell he liked that idea and wanted to stay.

"So what are we going to do about Morgan's body?" Alba asked.

"What can we do?" Holly asked. "We're not supposed to get involved."

"It's too late for that, we already are involved," I said.

The room let out a collective sigh as we all relaxed in silence while thinking about what could be done.

"Can her ghost come find us?" Alba finally asked me.

"I don't really know. That's why I'm here. Before I came here, we had people and ghosts traipsing in and out all the time wanting to talk to each other. My mom is a medium too, you know, so they were coming to see her. Sometimes ghosts would randomly find me on the street. It was weird and awkward. I never knew what to say, and

I never knew how they found my mother. I assume it was word of mouth. There's no way that Morgan's ghost would know to look for me specifically."

"Yeah, same," Holly agreed. "I have these – gifts, and I just don't know how to use them."

I rolled my eyes. I was so tired of hearing being a witch referred to as a *gift*. "Personally, I don't think being a witch is a *gift*. It's a curse is what it is."

"Mercy! How can you say such a thing!" Jax exclaimed. "It *is* a gift. Witches are a minority in this world."

"Jax, minorities are routinely discriminated against, why would I intentionally want to be a minority?"

"You can do something so few people can; you have the powers to speak to the *dead!* And Alba! She doesn't even have to break a sweat to move the furniture," she said with a little titter.

That made Alba smile. "The perks. What can I say?"

"Being a witch is so much more than just having these random powers. I think once we're done with college, we'll see how our powers really are gifts. I think you'll appreciate what you've been given someday," Jax added confidently.

"My God, you sound like my mother!" I cried as the black cat jumped up onto my lap and snuggled his soft face against the slope of my neck.

"Well, then your mother is right," Jax said with a laugh. "Maybe we should all go to class and learn a thing or two."

"I have to agree with Jax about that," I said, nodding

my head and jumping off the bed. I glanced down at my watch. "I've got Incantation class in fifteen."

Alba stood up too, "Holly and I should go, too. We both have Energy in Nature next."

"What are we going to do about Morgan?" I asked before Holly and Alba could reach the door.

"I have Ghost Science this afternoon. Maybe I'll figure out how to call her," Alba suggested. "I'll let you know at dinner."

CHAPTER TEN

Talk around the school about the Hartford girl's murder seemed to die down by the end of the week, but our little clique had managed to earn ourselves a nickname – The Witch Squad – after word spread that Sorceress Stone had disciplined us for our independent detective field work. Chatter about Friday night's social event with the school of wizardry next door replaced talk of the murder. I didn't give the social much thought; after all, I wasn't really in the market for a male companion. In fact, I hadn't been in the market for *any* companions whatsoever on the first day of school, but yet people seemed to have a way of finding me.

It had begun with my ooey-gooey sticky sweet roommate, Jax, which had somehow cultured into a bad rash resulting in blistery Alba, Holly was thrown in as an ornate bonus, and Sweets – well – I had to admit, was the icing on the cupcake. I mean, what wasn't to like when it came to Sweets? She was quiet, unassuming, unintentionally lovable, and she brought me treats.

In addition, I had also seemed to have inherited a cat. I'd named him Sneaks – only because he constantly managed to sneak into my dorm room whenever he could. No matter how many times I took him back outside, he always managed to sneak back inside. I hadn't been able to figure out yet who he belonged to, but I thought eventually someone had to come around knocking on doors looking for him – I mean he was a smart cat – *someone* had to be missing him. He seemed to be able to obey commands and when I talked to him; he actually appeared to listen. Something in his eyes seemed sympathetic, and I appreciated the quiet, content way about him.

Thursday after class, the Witch Squad drove down the hill into downtown Aspen Falls for a little girls shopping trip. Holly had convinced us all that we needed new outfits for the social, and she promised she'd put her fashion skills to good use and pick us each out something flattering. So when it was time to get dressed for the event Friday after class, we all had something nice to wear.

As usual, Holly found a way to make her breasts the star of her show. They were on full display, front and center in her tight little red dress. She had thrown on black heels and blown her hair out, and I had to admit, she was looking extremely hot, and perhaps I was slightly jealous.

I looked down at my cleavage. Holly had insisted I

lead with my chest and wear a boob shirt too. Unfortunately, the shirt hadn't come with the boobs. My little ladies didn't do much in the tight black top she'd picked out. But I could see how they looked better in the new shirt than the Pretty Reckless band t-shirt I'd have probably worn instead. She had wanted me to wear contacts for the occasion, but I thought I looked better in my glasses. I did allow her to put a little extra eye makeup on me, though, to accompany my usual dark eyeliner.

Jax had finally simmered down the witchy garb, but she couldn't seem to abandon the purple and black striped tights. Luckily, purple and black tights under a black mini dress actually looked kind of cute. Even with her pointy-toed black heels, she managed to make witch - cute. We had even convinced Jax to get rid of the orangey-red dye job, and she'd switched it up to a more normal platinum blonde.

Holly intentionally amped up Sweets' va-va-voom factor by stuffing her into a pair of black pleather pants and a garnet red corset top with a sweetheart neckline. Sweets had gone from a sweet sugarplum fairy to a BDSM seductress in the time it took to cinch up her girdle.

"The only thing that you're missing from that outfit is your whip," I told her with a little laugh.

"Is it too much?" she asked nervously.

How would I even begin to answer that question? "Too much what? Boob?"

"Too much anything?"

"There's certainly a lot of boob, that's for sure," I

answered, grinning broadly.

"You don't like it, do you?" she asked.

I could tell a lot was riding on my answer and I didn't want to hurt Sweets' feelings, so I went the neutral way. "You look hot," I said with a shrug. "You just don't look like the Sweets that I met in Witchcraft 101 four days ago."

A little giggle sprung to her lips. "Good!"

"Where's Alba?" Holly asked with a frown on her lips. "She's late for her makeover!"

"I'm pretty sure she stayed late to talk to Sorceress Stone about summoning ghosts. She said she might do that. Since I haven't had any luck calling Morgan's spirit, she's been trying to learn how to do it herself. I know she's been upset that we haven't been more help," I said. I felt pretty bad about not being able to help, too but I didn't know what else I could do.

Just then Holly's dorm room door flew open, and Alba strutted in, out of breath.

"Jeez, run all the way here?" I asked her with a little laugh.

"You're late!" Holly barked at Alba.

"I stayed late with the Sorceress. She was giving me some extra practice on summoning spirits."

"Why don't you just tell her what you're trying to do? She could summon Morgan's ghost," Jax suggested.

Alba shrugged as she threw her backpack down on the floor and fell into the oversized saucer chair next to her desk. "I don't know, I guess I figured if she wanted to do that – *if* she *can* do that – she would have by now. Why would I have to tell her to?"

Jax nodded. "Yeah, you're right. They say ghosts won't go to just anyone. They have to feel safe with the medium."

"Maybe Morgan just doesn't feel safe with us," Alba suggested with her head hung low.

"No, I bet she's trying to guard her body. Whoever stole it, stole it for a reason and I'm worried about what that reason might be," I told the squad.

"What reasons could there be?" Holly asked as she pulled her curling iron closer to Alba's chair.

"Obviously whatever intentions they have, they're evil."

"Duh," Alba uttered sarcastically. "Ow! Watch it!" she screamed as Holly began to tug on Alba's short hair.

"Sorry."

"I just wish I could figure out the weird feeling I got from Morgan's dad," I said regretfully.

"You still think he has something to do with her death?" Jax asked.

I shrugged. "I have no idea. There was just something about him that set off alarm bells in my body. I'm hoping it will come to me."

"Maybe we should all meditate on it," Jax suggested. She peered into the mirror and touched at her makeup.

Holly shook her head with a bobby pin in her mouth. "Uh-uh. Tonight isn't about work. Or school. It's about fun. We haven't had any fun all week."

"There's a dead girl out there with her body missing, and you're worried about fun?" Alba asked her wryly.

"I think she's right." I had to agree with Holly. What more was there for us to do? We were novice witches with no right to be involved, even though we all wanted to help. "Let's just take the opportunity to meet the men tonight. Maybe we'll pick up on something from them. We can't rule them out, ya know." Libby and Cinder's words replayed in my mind – around here you have to consider *everyone* a suspect.

At 7 o'clock the five of us wandered down the stairs, out the lobby, and into the courtyard. An assortment of mostly well-dressed men were strolling around, drinking cups of punch and looking like a bunch of aristocratic sons.

Ugh. I was so not the 'marry a politician' sort of girl. I had hoped there would be more normal guys here. My attention was drawn to a squabble going on towards the left side of the courtyard. One of the Wiz Kids – as I'd learned most of the witches called the guys next door – was arguing with one of the girls from my school about whether or not the girls had cheated at the recent Broomery Golf tournament.

Holly immediately abandoned the squad for a nice looking boy with an expensive looking ring on his pinky finger and an ascot around his neck that introduced himself as Evan. Alba excused herself to find a plate of food, leaving Jax, Sweets, and myself to wander the courtyard awkwardly. I felt like a high school girl trying to find a lunch table to sit at again. Finally I suggested we just take a seat and people watch for awhile.

"Oooh, he's cute," Jax commented on a tall, thin boy

wearing a simple pair of khaki pants and a short sleeve button down shirt.

"At least he's not wearing a suit," I agreed. "The rest of these guys look like business majors, not at all what I would expect for a school of wizardry."

Libby and Cinder joined us; each was wearing a nice dress and high heels. "Well, the men are told to dress their best for these social events," Libby told us.

"I figured as much, but does their best really have to be a suit and tie? I'd rather see everyone in jeans and a t-shirt. Dressing realistically is much more indicative of their true personalities." It just didn't make sense to me. And it was quite disappointing if I were being honest.

"Maybe some of them feel most comfortable in a suit and tie?" Sweets suggested lightly.

I shrugged. "I guess that's possible. But the man of *my* dreams certainly won't be wearing a suit and tie?"

"Will he be wearing a cowboy hat and boots?" Sweets asked coyly.

"What?" I asked her, confused.

She pointed her finger across the courtyard, where a small group of men had just walked in. None of them wore suits or ties; instead, they all wore denim jeans and an assortment of nice shirts. One of them wore jeans, a button down plaid shirt and a cowboy hat and cowboy boots and for some reason he seemed to hold my attention and I could hardly pull my eyes away.

The girls and I watched as the small group of men made their way through the crowd, stopping to chat with people here and there. Finally, they broke free of the big crowd and made their way to the shallow end, near us. My heart began to thump nervously in my chest. The cowboy was a handsome man, tall, square jaw line, broad shoulders, and muscular arms. Something about him set my skin on fire.

"Hello ladies," said the man next to the cowboy. He was a tall, gangly fellow with a shock of blonde hair that fell into his eyes when he turned his head.

"Hi there," Jax said with a big smile. "I'm Jax; this is Sweets, Mercy, Libby and Cinder."

The tall fellow shook Jax's hand and kissed the top of it causing Jax to giggle. "It's nice to meet you, Jax. I'm Freddy. This is Houston, Nick, Juan, and Curt."

"Nice to meet you all," Jax smiled at them all. "Are you all first-year students?"

"As a matter of fact, we are," Freddy said with a nice little smile. "And you ladies?"

"We're second year," Libby said, pointing at her and her sister.

"The rest of us are first year," said Jax.

The music blaring from the speakers changed, and suddenly it was playing a casual slow song.

"Would any of you care to dance?" Freddy asked, looking directly at Jax.

She lunged forward, taking the hand he had extended towards her. "Absolutely. See ya ladies!" she called back to us as Freddy pulled her out onto the dance floor, leaving us alone with his four friends.

"I like your hat," I said to Houston, the cowboy, as we all stood looking at each other awkwardly.

He touched the brim, nodding at me in the process. "Thanks."

"I've never met a cowboy wizard before," Sweets said with a little giggle.

"Just because he has a cowboy hat doesn't make him a cowboy. Are you a cowboy?" I asked him. I would be surprised if he were. I'd never seen a cowboy wizard before either.

A slow, shy smile spread across his face, and one eyebrow shot up. "Would you like me to be a cowboy?"

Ah. He was a player. I'd met those kinds of guys before. Immediately I stood up. The night was quickly tanking. "You be whatever trips your trigger, Cowboy," I said curtly before heading back towards Winston Hall. I was going to grab a bagel and a macchiato from the coffee shop and call it a night. Maybe Sneaks would be back, and I could snuggle up with him and a spell book or my Kindle or something.

I hadn't gotten within ten feet of the hall when I heard the distinct sound of boots pounding the cobblestone behind me. In seconds the tall, good-looking cowboy had situated himself between me and the door to the girls' lobby. "Well hold up there, now."

I stopped and looked up at him in annoyance. "Lose your horse?" I asked him sarcastically.

"Why'd you run off so quick?" he asked casually. "I was only playing."

"Well, that's the thing, Cowboy; I'm not really into games."

"I'm not either," he promised, holding his hands up

as if swearing an oath. "My buddies were just giving me a hard time about wearing a cowboy hat and boots to the social, and when the first thing you noticed was the hat, well, I didn't know if it was a good thing or a bad thing."

I was quiet for a moment. I guess that made sense. I let a little smile curl the side of my mouth.

Houston put one arm up on the doorway and leaned in a little closer to me. "So, is the hat a good thing or a bad thing?"

I shrugged as color flooded my face. "It's different. I happen to have a soft spot for different."

"So that means it's good?" he asked. His hazel eyes sparkled as he looked at me.

"I suppose, if you must put a label on it, yeah, the hat's good," I admitted.

He stood up straighter. "Well alright then, can we start over?"

I couldn't help but appreciate his little southern drawl; it was pretty cute. "What the heck, sure."

"Good. Let me properly introduce myself. I'm Houston Brooks. Yes. I am a cowboy. I grew up in Texas. My mother says I was conceived in Houston, which a-course I never really needed to know, but that's where she came up with the name."

Nothing like knowing where a guy was conceived to break the ice. "It's nice to meet you, Houston, I'm Mercy Habernackle. I'm from Illinois. I have no idea where I was conceived."

He chuckled. "It sure is a pleasure to meet you Mercy Habernackle. You've got beautiful green eyes, they are very bewitching," he said quietly as a little smile played around his lips.

I felt my cheeks redden again at the compliment. I wasn't used to getting compliments. "Thanks, Houston."

"You can call me Hugh, most folks do. Would you like to dance?" he asked me.

I looked around behind me and saw that all of my friends were on the dance floor. "I'm really not much of a dancer," I admitted nervously.

"It's alright, it's slow dancing, not advanced algebra," he said with a chuckle.

"I'm probably better at advanced algebra than slow dancing, but ok," I said, grinning up at him. He extended his elbow to me, and I slipped my hand through it and let him lead me to the dance floor. He turned to me and soon I felt his arms slip around my back, pulling me closer to him. My pulse started to race, and I awkwardly tried to keep time with him, but my legs and feet just didn't want to communicate properly with my brain.

"Boy, you were right," he whispered into my ear as we circled the dance floor. "You really can't dance, can you?"

I dug my fingers into his shoulder playfully. "I told you!"

"Have you eaten? How about we get a bite to eat?"

I wondered if he'd felt the rumbling in my stomach while we danced. "Yeah, food would be good. I'm starving."

"They've got free pizza tonight in our lobby. Can I tempt you away for a slice?"

I looked at my dancing friends. The thought that I should probably let them know that I was wandering off with a stranger for a few minutes alerted me to the fact that I was being invited into the boys' building. Perhaps I'd find a clue about the Hartford girl's missing body. "Yeah, let me just let my friends know where I'm going. I'll be right back," I said quickly.

"Ok, I'll wait over here," Hugh said and left the dance floor.

I scuttled over to Jax quickly, who was still cutting a rug with Freddy. "Jax, I'm going to go get a slice of pizza with Houston in the lobby of the boys' dorm."

She nodded as she spun around to the new fast beat. "Ok Merc, see ya later!"

The boys' lobby looked much like the girls'. Except they had a big screen TV and a lounge area where our coffee shop was.

"So what brings you to The Institute, Mercy?" Houston asked as he slid two slices of pepperoni pizza onto a paper plate.

"Truth?" I asked with a little smirk.

He looked up at me and smiled. "Yeah, the truth."

"It was either this or a correctional facility." I felt bad leading with the truth. Holly had specifically forbidden me from saying anything such as this, but I had no interest in meeting someone and then them finding out my worst secrets later and then ditching me. I'd had that happen far too many times in my lifetime to want to start that here where the playing field was level.

"A correctional facility? What did you do?" I noticed

that his eyes crinkled in the corner when he smiled. It was pretty adorable.

I shrugged as I grabbed us each a napkin from the counter. "I was born a witch."

He led us to a table and chairs in the lobby. He pulled my chair out for me and pushed me in when I sat down. I'd never had anyone do that for me in the past; it made me feel a bit like a lady. *If he's going to treat you like a lady, then act like one!* I heard my mother's voice in my head.

He sat down across the table from me and took his hat off, setting it on the chair next to him. His sandy blonde hair curled up around his ears. "Yeah, being born with – powers – isn't really as easy as many would like to believe. We can't do *everything*, but we can do just enough to make us different."

I nodded. "Exactly. I'm really hoping that The Institute will teach me how to use my abilities effectively, and I never thought I'd say this, but, I've enjoyed meeting a group of girls who are witches too. No one judges here. It's actually kind of refreshing."

Hugh nodded. "I'm glad you're having a good experience here."

"Aren't you?"

He looked down at his plate. "It's alright. Being in a dorm full of guys, in classes full of guys, and having dinner with a bunch of guys, has been rather – boring. This is kind of nice, though."

His hazel eyes looked at me intently. *Wow, this guy is good.* I smiled at him as a little shiver zipped down my spine and pebbled my skin.

"It's kind of chilly in here," I said when my goose bumps wouldn't go away.

"You're cold? I have a sweater in my room. I could go get you one?" he asked, about to stand up.

I reached out an arm and pulled him back down. "No, no. It's fine. Maybe we could just finish our pizza outside? You must have your air conditioner on in here. You're lucky. We don't have air in our dorms."

He shook his head as he finished the slice he was working on. "No, we don't have air either," he said and then stood up. "Let's go outside. It's a nice evening."

I smiled at him, and together we walked back into the courtyard. As we passed through the short stone wall, I heard a scream come from the dance floor. "That sounded like Jax!" I said, handing Houston my plate of pizza. "Can you take this please?"

I took off towards the dance floor and saw Alba rushing towards the dance floor from the cafeteria. "Jax!" she hollered.

CHAPTER ELEVEN

"Jax! What happened?" I asked as I found the blonde pixie haired girl on the dance floor with a look of horror on her face.

The rest of the Witch Squad had circled her too. Jax pointed at Freddy. "This creep practically molested me on the dance floor!"

Alba's temper flared. "He got rough with you?"

Jax nodded emphatically. "Yeah, we were just dancing and then all of a sudden he's got his tongue down my throat! I tried to push him off of me, but he wouldn't budge and then before I knew it he had his filthy paws where they shouldn't have been."

Freddy's hands went up in defense as Alba's sturdy frame challenged him immediately. "Hey, hey. I thought the chick wanted it."

"What part of stop did you not understand, jerk!" Jax

hollered at him.

Suddenly Houston was by my side. "What happened?"

I looked up at him angrily. "Your *friend* happened. Come on Jax, let's go."

"Wait, Mercy, don't go," Houston pleaded as he looked between Freddy, Jax, Alba and me.

Sweets and Holly left their dance partners to follow Alba and me as we escorted Jax back to Winston Hall. "Are you alright Jax?" I asked as we all plopped down onto the sofa and arm chairs in a little nook in the lobby.

She nodded with tear filled eyes. "Yeah, we were having so much fun and then all of a sudden it's like he snapped and he got super aggressive! I didn't do anything, I swear."

Alba shook her head; her dark eyes blazed angrily. "You don't have to apologize. It's not your fault he got handsy with you. That jerk. He should be kicked out of school for that."

Jax wiped at her eyes. "It's ok, Alba. Don't get him in trouble. I learned my lesson; that's all."

"You should have just zapped him one," Holly said angrily. "Guys like that need to be taught a lesson."

"Yeah, let's go back to the room and curse him good," I said with a little nod.

Jax dropped her head into her hands and began to sob.

"Jax! What's the matter?" Sweets asked, rubbing Jax's back.

"Don't cry," said Holly. "Let's get even!"

"I can't get even!" Jax finally sobbed.

"What do you mean?" I asked her. I looked at the other girls and searched their faces to see if they knew what she was talking about.

"I can't do a spell on Freddy!"

"Ok, you don't have to. We were just trying to make you feel better," I assured her.

"No, you don't understand," she bawled. "I *want* to put a spell on Freddy, but I can't!"

The rest of the girls and I looked at each other in confusion. "You're not making any sense, Jax," I told her.

She pulled her head out of her hands and sat up, looking around at us. Tears covered her cheeks, and her makeup was smeared under her eyes. "I have something to confess."

"Confess? About Freddy?" Alba asked her.

She shook her head. "No, not about Freddy. About me."

We all exchanged nervous glances as Jax took a deep breath.

"I can't do spells," she finally admitted.

A long pause followed as we each took in her words. Finally, I spoke slowly. "That's ok; you'll learn to do them this year."

She shook her head. "I can't do *anything*. I have no powers. I'm – I'm – I'm not a witch." She looked between us quickly as if her words were suddenly going to alienate each of us.

Sweets and Holly sucked in their breath. Alba and I looked at each other, our eyes wide open in shock.

"You're *not* a witch?" I asked, unsure if what I'd just heard was correct. The witchiest witch here was not a witch? Maybe I needed the wax cleaned out of my ears.

She shook her head from side to side. "Uh-uh."

Alba looked at her curiously. "Then why are you here?"

Jax threw herself back onto the sofa and covered her face with her hands. "Because I want to *be* a witch!"

"Yeah, well, I want to *be* Taylor Momsen, but I don't go to band camp to do it!" I snarked at her.

Sweets shot me a disapproving glance. "Mercy! That's not helping Jax."

"What? She's not a witch, and she's at *witch* college. Last time I checked, they weren't handing out witch cards at the door."

"So? She's here for a reason, I'm sure," Sweets said and then turned to Jax. "Why do you want to be a witch, Jax?"

"You guys wouldn't understand," she whined.

Holly rubbed Jax's knee. "Try us, sweetie."

Jax sat up slowly. "My mother is a witch. My aunt is a witch. My grandmother was a witch. All the women in my family are witches. Do you know how awful it is to go through life with all your family being a witch and you're *not*? I've been waiting my whole life to come into my powers. And they've never come. I've given up hope that they are *ever* coming. I'm just a girl," she finished quietly, her voice cracking at the end.

"I can't believe this. All this time I've been your roommate and you never told me," I said to her. I felt deceived. At least back home, I knew I was the only witch in the room. But now my roommate was intentionally deceiving us about her true identity.

"I didn't want you to treat me differently," Jax cried.

"That's not fair, Jax," I hollered. "You didn't even give me a chance to treat you normally. Besides, I'd give *anything* not to be a witch. I didn't *ask* for this. I didn't ask for any of this. And you get to be normal. And what do you do? You dress like a lunatic, show up at witch college and *pretend* to be something you're not! You're a little girl playing dress up, and it's ridiculous quite honestly!" Something inside me begged me to stop, but I couldn't help it. "I don't even understand how they let you in. This is the *Paranormal* Institute for Witches. You barely qualify for *normal*, much less *paranormal!*"

Holly and Sweets looked at me with sadness in their eyes. I knew I had taken it too far. Even Alba didn't look pleased with my little rant.

Jax's expression fell, and with it, my heart. I hadn't meant to be so vicious towards her. I knew I had a lot of pent up anger for being born a witch. It hadn't been fair, but it also hadn't been Jax's fault. My rant hadn't been about her. It had been about me. I looked down at the hands in my lap. I dug my thumbnail into the fleshy webbed skin between my thumb and my first finger, hoping the pain would keep me from crying. With sadness in my eyes, I looked up and made eye contact with Jax.

The pain was there. I had hurt her badly. My stomach flipped, and I suddenly felt nauseous about the horrible things I'd said and how I'd made Jax feel.

"Jax, I-," I began. But it was too late. She stood up, tears streaming down her face and rushed out of the room.

Holly and Sweets jumped up and began to run after her, but she pushed them away. "Go away," she screamed.

"Jax, wait, let us come with you," Holly cried.

The sound of Jax's heels clicking on the tile floor diminished little by little as she ran down the hallway. Holly and Sweets came back to me and joined Alba in giving me dirty looks.

"That was so mean, Mercy," Holly barked.

I hung my head in shame. She was absolutely right. "I know...I," I began.

"So mean," Sweets chimed in.

"And here I thought we were labeling *me* the bitchy witch," Alba said in turn. "Looks like it takes one to know one."

"Guys, I'm sorry. I know. I'm terrible. I should have never said those awful things. I feel horrible. It's just - my life hasn't been all flying broomsticks and cute shoes. Being a witch has been horrible for me. I've been teased and tortured my entire life. And when I finally started using my powers to help me out of sticky situations, it would backfire, and *I'd* get in trouble. People have looked at me as a bad person my entire life. I guess I just don't know how to be a *good person*."

"Jax is a really good person," Sweets said sadly.

"I know she is. I took that all too far. It's just that she

has what I've always wanted. She's just a girl. I've always wanted to be just a girl. And to hear that she'd been lying to us all this time…"

"She didn't want us to treat her the way that you've been treated your whole life," Sweets pointed out.

I hung my head again. "I'm so embarrassed. I feel horrible. I'll find her. I'll make it right," I promised, standing up and heading down the hallway.

I took off down the hall with the rest of the squad close behind. We poked our head into room after room to no avail.

"Jax!" I called as I walked down the stone-walled corridors.

Door after door we opened and couldn't find her. My heart sunk at the damage that I'd caused. We retreated back to our room that evening without her.

"What are we going to do?" Sweets worried as ten o'clock came and went, and Jax still hadn't returned.

"She'll come back," I assured her. "She's just upset. She'll come back in the night, and I'll apologize and make things right, I promise."

I felt like an overprotective mother as I lay awake that night waiting for my child to come home – to call – to anything, just to let me know she was okay. The rest of the girls had gone back to their own rooms, and I lay in my bed, cuddling with Sneaks, waiting for Jax to come back.

"Oh Sneaks, I feel just terrible for being so mean to Jax," I lamented. "This is all my fault."

Sneaks rubbed his soft dark fur against my skin,

sending goosebumps careening across my arms. "Gosh, I've got goosebumps again. I just can't seem to warm up around here," I told him as I pulled a blanket up from the foot of the bed and wrapped myself in it.

I began to shiver even more. "Jeez, the last time I had shivers like this, was the first day of school and it turned out that Hartford girl was …" I stopped midsentence. She had been dead. The thought finally registered with me. My shivers were a sign. My spidey senses were tingling again, and Jax was missing. "Oh Sneaks, I'm so worried about Jax. Maybe I should go wake Sorceress Stone to help me find her."

Just then there was a knock at the door. I shot out of bed and lurched forward into the dark inkiness of my dorm room. Jax was back! "Oh thank God, finally, you're…"

But it wasn't Jax at my door. It was Holly, and by the look on her face, I thought she'd seen the devil.

"Holly! What in the world are you doing here at midnight?" I asked her as I turned around to look at the clock on my desk. I peered back at her in my doorway curiously. I could see she'd come with Alba.

"Mercy. Oh, my gosh, you've got to let us in. It's Jax!"

CHAPTER TWELVE

"Jax?" My heart began to beat faster; I could hear it thumping in my ears. "You saw Jax? Where? When? Where is she?"

Holly pushed herself into my room, and Alba followed right behind her. Holly looked at Alba nervously.

"You've got to tell her," Alba commanded her.

Holly took a deep breath and then told me what she had seen. "I saw her in my dream. She was walking outside, and a man came up from behind her and grabbed her. She struggled with him, but he was too strong. Mercy, Jax has been kidnapped!"

"You're sure?" I asked as I felt my food start to move in my stomach. It felt like I was going to be sick and the shivers wouldn't stop pebbling my arms and legs. I knew she was sure; I knew that's what my senses were telling me and that was why Jax hadn't come home yet for me to apologize to her.

"I'm sure," Holly said nervously.

"We've got to call the police," I decided. I pulled a sweatshirt off the chair next to my bed and pulled it on.

Alba shook her head. "We have to tell Sorceress Stone. She'll throw a fit if we call the police but didn't report Jax missing to start with."

"I feel like Sorceress Stone doesn't like Jax. What if she tells us we can't report it? What if she doesn't do anything about it? We can't let Jax meet the same fate that Morgan Hartford did," I argued.

"I'm so freaked out right now," said Holly. She hopped up on Jax's desk and absent-mindedly grabbed a snow globe off the side of her desk that belonged to Jax. Flipping it over she gave it a good shake and then turned it right side up and watched as tiny little golden leaves fell over the miniature town of Aspen Falls. Suddenly her body stiffened, and her eyes stared across the room blankly.

"Holly?" Alba asked nervously.

Holly didn't respond. With the globe in her hands, she didn't move. It was as if she were in a trance.

I touched her knee. "Holly, wake up."

Alba held her hand up as if to stop me. "Maybe she's having a vision."

We watched as Holly's body shook while her eyelids fluttered open and then closed and then open again. "Jax!" escaped from her lips as she finally lost whatever possession had been holding her and she crumpled to the desk.

"Alba, grab her!" I hollered as I shot forward to grab her before she tumbled off the desk. We both got an arm around her and pulled her off the desk, sitting her down on the bed carefully.

"Holly, wake up," Alba said, shaking her gruffly.

Her eyes fluttered open. She looked straight ahead for a moment, before catching her bearings and then looking around to find us staring at her nervously.

"Are you alright, Holly?" I asked.

"I saw Jax," she announced immediately. "She's alive."

"Where is she?" Alba asked.

"She's being held somewhere. I saw her. Her arms were tied, and her mouth was gagged. Oh my gosh guys, she's so scared. We've got to find her."

"Did you see anyone there with her?" I asked.

Holly shook her head. "I didn't see anyone."

"When you had your dream earlier, could you see who took her?" Alba asked.

"It was a man. I only saw the back of his head. I couldn't see his face."

It was obvious between the dream and the premonition she just had; Holly was rattled. "Are you going to be ok?" I asked her.

She nodded but held her hand out to stare at her wobbly hand. "Yeah, but I'm kind of shaky do you have anything to drink?"

I opened the small mini fridge and pulled out a little bottle of orange juice. "Here, it's Jax's."

I slipped on my sneakers while Holly guzzled the juice. "We have to tell Sorceress Stone. There's no way around it," I told Alba.

"Ok, I don't even know where to find her," Alba said with a little grunt.

"We'll check the lobby and see if there's anyone down there. If we can't find her, then we'll just have to call the police ourselves."

Holly stood up. She was wobbly on her feet, but quickly she gained her bearings.

"Come on ladies," I said. "We don't have much time."

Sneaks tried to follow me out the door, but for once I didn't want to let him go. If we didn't find Jax soon and something happened to her, I'd need the comfort when I got back.

"Sorry, Sneaks. You stay here for now. It's safer here," I said and shut the door behind me.

The three of us raced down the stairs and to the lobby. No one was around, and there wasn't even an emergency phone number posted anywhere. We had no idea how to reach Sorceress Stone.

"We're just going to have to call the police," I said. "We can't wait any longer."

As I dug my cell phone out of my back pocket, Holly and Alba saw a shadow cross in front of the doors leading to the courtyard. "Did you see that?" Holly asked.

Alba nodded. "Yeah, I wonder who is up wandering around outside at this hour?"

"Do you think it's Jax? Maybe she got away,"

suggested Holly. She chewed on her fingernails nervously.

"I doubt that it's Jax. Why would she be running away from the building? I think we should go see who it is. It could be her kidnapper," I rationalized. My heart was in my stomach as the three of us snuck to the edge of the darkened wall and then slid against the wall to the glass doors and peered outside.

"I can't see anything," Holly whispered.

"Shhh," I hissed. "Whoever it is will hear you!"

"They're outside, they aren't going to hear me," Holly whispered back.

"Who's not going to hear you?" a voice suddenly asked from behind us.

Alba, Holly and I jumped, letting a startled scream out. We turned around to find none other than Sweets in her bathrobe and a pair of fuzzy bunny slippers holding a snack from the vending machine.

"Sweets! You scared the crap out of me!" I hissed at her.

"What in the hell are you doing down here?" Alba cursed.

Sweets shrank down before shrugging and eyed her honey bun. "I was hungry."

"Well, for goodness sake, be quiet, we're on a stake out," Holly whispered.

Sweets squatted down low, mirroring our stances and peered out the window with us. "Who are we looking for?"

"Jax's kidnapper!" Holly told her.

Sweets' eyes grew large. "Jax has been kidnapped?"

Holly nodded. "Yes. And we just saw a suspicious figure walk past these doors."

Her eyes grew even larger. "You think it's her kidnapper?"

"It could be. We're going to have to go out there and check. Why don't Alba and I go? Holly, you and Sweets stay here in case we need you to call for help."

Holly and Sweets nodded. They were obviously happy not to have to go out where the kidnapper was.

"What are we going to do out there?" I asked Alba.

She shrugged. "I have no idea. Wing it!"

"Ok, let's go," I whispered and followed behind her as she quietly slid the courtyard, door open wide enough so we could squeeze out.

Alba led the way as we walked out into the slightly illuminated darkness. The dull glow from the street lamps surrounding the courtyard revealed nothing. There was no one in the courtyard and it was hard to see past the short stone walls surrounding the cobblestone area. Alba pointed towards the sidewalk to our right, the direction in which we'd seen the dark figure moving through the window.

Without a word, I followed her closely, my heart pounded like a canon in my ears, making the silence of the night loud and scary. I looked back and saw the dark shadowy outline of Sweets and Holly watching through the window. Alba moved forward quickly, crouching low to the ground. I couldn't help but think about the fact that she moved quite stealthily for a woman of her size.

We clung to the darkness and shadows of the building as we made our way around Winston Hall and towards the Canterbury Building, a building that we had had many of our witch classes in over the past week. The sidewalk split in two at the stairs of the old building, wrapping around it, we had to make a decision on which way to go. Alba pointed to her left and then pointed to me and to our right. She wanted me to investigate on my own. Panicking, my head shook vigorously from side to side. Alba's eyes narrowed on me, and she pointed staunchly to her right, wordlessly insisting that I venture that way on my own.

As Alba headed in the opposite direction, I reluctantly turned around, facing the darkness head on. With my heart in my throat, I took a dozen steps forward and then the sound of a man's voice rode past me with a gust of wind. I stopped dead in my tracks. Terror gripped my body. I wanted to turn around and scream for Alba to come back, but my body was paralyzed with fear. What if that man was the one that had taken Jax? And what if the man that had taken Jax had been the one to kill Morgan?

As I debated what to do, I stood there with my eyes closed engulfed in black, trying to sink into a safer state of denial, when suddenly I felt an energy whoosh past my body. It felt different than the wind, but maybe it was the wind. I felt my long hair lift off of my shoulders and dance around my face. My eyes shot open, searching for a sign of what I was feeling, but saw nothing. I continued to hear the sound of a man's voice, chanting off in the distance.

Against my will, I found my legs carrying me forward, towards the chanting. As trees began to clear, I could see a colorful swirling of lights floating off in the distance. I had never gone this far on the campus, and I wondered what I would find up ahead. I wished that Alba and I wouldn't have split up.

The cobblestone path ended at a rickety picket fence. There was a gate at the end of the path, so I assumed it was part of the campus property, but perhaps wasn't for student use. The chanting and energy field was coming from inside of the picket fence. I knew if I wanted to find out who the man was and what was going on, I'd have to be brave and open the gate.

I put one hand on the gate and suddenly a body appeared behind me out of the darkness and touched my shoulders. My body convulsed in fear as I spun around to see Alba. I had never been so scared, yet so relieved in my entire life. "Alba! You scared the hell out of me!" I hollered in a whisper at her.

"Shhh," she hissed with a finger to her lips.

"Sorry. You literally just about gave me a heart attack."

"Do you hear that?" she asked me quietly.

I nodded my head. "I've been following the sound. It sounds like a man is chanting. And check out the light show."

"Yeah, it's coming from in here," she said and pointed towards the fenced in area.

"We can't go in there," I told her nervously.

"We have to. That's probably Jax's kidnapper. We've

got to find her."

My head lowered. I knew she was right. I took a deep breath and sucked up as much moxie as I could muster and unlatched the gate. Alba went through first, and I followed closely on her heels, holding her arm for protection.

"Stop being such a baby," she shot at me quietly.

"I can't help it. This is freaking me out," I told her as we walked through the cool grass which led down into a valley. As the trees cleared and the moon lit the wide expanse of space that we'd just wandered into, it was immediately evident where we were.

"It's a graveyard!" I whispered in surprise. Who would have thought the campus would have a graveyard right here?

"Shh," Alba said again. "The lights are coming from over here."

We followed the lights, winding our way through a row of tombstones. The man's voice became clearer the closer we got, and the energy that rode on the wind grew stronger. "Can you feel the energy circling the light show?" I whispered to Alba as my hair danced around my shoulders.

She nodded and squeezed my arm, silencing me. When we got close enough, our two darkened figures slid down behind a large headstone. We peered off to the side of the tombstone. There was a small garden shed or perhaps a mausoleum at the base of the valley. A man was standing on a short altar in front of it with his arms wide open to the heavens, chanting in a foreign tongue.

"What's he saying?" I asked her.

"It sounds like Latin," she whispered back.

"I can't see his face," I murmured. "If only he'd turn around."

As if on command, the man suddenly stopped chanting. He lowered his arms, and the swirling colorful lights disintegrated into the night sky, leaving only the illumination of the moon behind. My hair dropped to my shoulders as the wind let it out of its grasp and silence filled the air around us, making me almost scared to breathe. Alba and I froze, afraid to move, lest we give away our positions.

The man dropped his head and turned around. I couldn't see his face, but his body was distinctively familiar – he was short and round and oddly cartoonish. As he lifted his head, the moon glared off his balding scalp and finally I got a good look at his face. I sucked in my breath. I knew who it was!

CHAPTER THIRTEEN

The mysterious man summoning the spirits was none other than Seymour, the janitor that I had seen on the first day on campus. I had all but forgotten about him. And then it hit me. I had spent the last week trying to figure out who Morgan's father resembled, and now here it was, it was Seymour. The two men both had the same dark curly hair and dark eyes. Morgan's father was quite a bit taller than Seymour, but their faces bore a striking resemblance to each other.

I squeezed Alba's arm, and then clapped a hand over my mouth, forcing myself to stay silent. I was afraid to talk. Afraid he'd hear us.

Seymour lifted his arms up high above his head and stretched them. He moved his head from side to side as if he were cracking his neck. Finally, he leaned over and picked up a shovel and a big tarp that were lying next to his feet and carried them inside the little building he was standing in front of. My eyes grew huge. This man was a wizard of some sort, and he had a shovel. Immediately I wondered if that was where he was holding Jax.

"That's the janitor! We've got to get in that building Alba, that could be where Jax is!" I whispered to her when I was sure Seymour was out of earshot in the building.

"You think he's the kidnapper?"

"He's obviously some sort of wizard. He's summoning the spirits. He's definitely up to something."

"Yeah, for sure he's up to something," Alba agreed.

"Do you think that he looks like Morgan's father? Makes me wonder if they are related."

Alba nodded. "It's dark, but I can sort of see the resemblance."

"We've got to get into that shed," I told Alba. "I'm almost positive that Jax is in there."

She shook her head. "No way. This is as far as we go. We need to report Jax missing, and we need to tell Detective Whitman our suspicions about this guy."

"Yeah, we need to get out of here before he comes back," I said.

"Come on," she whispered, leading me back into the darkness.

The race back to Winston Hall was a blur. Once we passed through the cemetery gate, we took off like shots in the night, firing through the pitch black sky back to the safety of our dormitory. Sweets and Holly were waiting for us in the lobby. Holly was nervously chewing on her fingernails and Sweets was devouring another sugary snack from the vending machine.

"Did you see anything?" Holly asked the minute we entered the building.

Alba and I bent over, gasping for breath. The intense sprint had kicked my butt, and I suddenly wished I'd brought my inhaler with me to college as my mom had reminded me. Gosh, I hated it when she was right.

Alba sucked in a deep breath and then looked at Sweets, who was still dressed in her robe and house slippers. "Sweets, we are going to need you to drive us to the police station. Now."

***

The ride to the station was just as intense as the stakeout had been. We described in detail everything we had seen and my suspicions about Seymour. As Sweets drove, I pulled out my phone and clicked on my Google app.

"What are you doing?" Alba asked me curiously.

"I'm looking up Morgan's obituary in the paper. I've got to know if there is any relationship between Seymour and Morgan's father."

I typed 'Morgan Hartford Aspen Falls obituary' into the search engine and clicked on the link from the Aspen Falls Observer. I scanned the obituary until I got to the list of people she was survived by. There in black and white, my suspicions were confirmed.

"Says here that Morgan Hartford is survived by her parents, Roger and Mary Hartford and her uncle, Seymour Hartford. Knew it!"

"Good call, Mercy," Holly cheered while we drove the short distance into Aspen Falls.

"The custodian is Morgan's uncle? Why would her uncle kill her?" Sweets asked.

I shook my head. "I don't know, but you've got to admit it's awfully suspicious that Seymour is a dead girl's uncle and he's the custodian of the school where another girl was just abducted."

Sweets nodded as she drove through the darkness, her eyes widened frightfully. "I just can't believe Jax has been abducted. I'm so worried about her. I hope she's alright."

"Me too," Holly lamented.

"We all do," I agreed. "But we're going to find her, don't worry."

The Aspen Falls Police Department was quiet when we arrived shortly after one o'clock in the morning. The front desk clerk looked more than a little surprised to see a group of women in their pajamas come rushing in at such an odd hour.

"May I help you?" he asked blandly, his bushy eyebrows slid together as he peered at us through the bullet-proof glass in the lobby.

"We have an emergency situation. Is Detective Whitman around?" I asked.

"No, Detective Whitman will be back tomorrow morning. What kind of emergency situation are we dealing with ladies?"

Holly threw herself at the glass in her little baby doll nightgown. "Oh officer, it's just terrible. Our friend has been abducted."

The officer paid Holly's flair for the dramatic no mind, but instead focused on what she'd said. "Someone's been abducted?"

We all nodded.

"My roommate," I added.

"You witnessed her being taken?" he asked.

I shook my head. "No, not exactly. She stormed off early tonight really, but Holly here, had a dream, and…"

"So you don't know that she's been taken?" he asked, attempting to clarify the situation.

"No, I *do* know she's been taken," I stated firmly.

"How do you know she's been taken?" he asked.

"Because Holly here, had a dream, and…" I repeated.

"Ok, stop. How long has your friend been missing?" he asked.

"Since about 8 o'clock," I said with a nod.

"She's only been gone about 5 hours?" he asked, looking at his watch.

I nodded. "Yes, but…"

"Ok, she's only been gone for 5 hours, you saw her walk off, I don't think this is an abduction case," the officer said, looking down at the paperwork he was working on. It was obvious he wanted to get back to whatever mundane drudgery he had been working on before we got there.

"You don't understand, officer. We also have

information regarding Morgan Hartford's killer," Alba added pointedly.

That caused the office to look up sharply. "What did you just say?"

"We know who Morgan Hartford's killer is," Alba repeated.

"Can you give me a moment?" he asked and then quickly walked into an office out of our range of vision.

"What are we going to do? They don't even care that Jax has been abducted," Sweets asked, wringing her hands.

"Our only hope is for Detective Whitman to get down here. He'll believe us." I was sure that it was true. He was our only hope for getting Jax back.

The officer returned to the window. "Ok, you can come on back," he said and buzzed us into the door on our right.

He met us inside and guided us to an office with an empty desk and office chair and two cushioned chairs in front of the desk. "I'll get a few more chairs." He brought in two more chairs, and the four of us took a seat. "I've called Detective Whitman. He's on his way down to the station. Can I get you ladies anything to drink or eat?"

"I'd take one of those donuts I saw when we came in," Sweets said with a little smile. We all looked at her. She'd just had a honey bun and a bear claw back in the lobby. "What? I'm a stress eater."

The officer brought Sweets a donut and the rest of us accepted a cup of coffee while we waited for Detective Whitman to arrive.

Finally, almost a half hour later, he made an appearance. "Girls, you're back. I should have known. What's going on?" he asked, as he took a seat behind the desk.

"My roommate has been abducted," I told him. I knew he'd believe us.

"Your roommate has been abducted? Who is your roommate?"

"Jax," I said and then suddenly realized I didn't even know my roommate's last name.

"Jax who?" he asked, taking notes on a yellow steno pad.

I looked from girl to girl for help and was met with blank stares. "Gosh, I honestly don't know that I've ever asked Jax her last name," I replied honestly. "It's only the first week of school."

"Uh-huh," he said. "Tell me exactly what happened."

I went through the whole scenario of the social event and how Freddy had been manhandling Jax, causing her to get upset. I even told him that Jax and I had gotten into an argument and she'd stormed off and she'd never come back.

"So, really, you don't *know* that your roommate has been abducted," he said, trying to lead me into admitting that it was possible that Jax was just hiding somewhere.

"No, Detective Whitman, we *know* that Jax has been abducted," Holly told him pointedly.

"How do you *know* this?"

"You know that we're, uh-hum, *witches*, right?" Holly began nervously.

A smile crept across the detective's face. "Yes, I do," he strung out slowly.

"Ok, well, sometimes witches know things that others don't," she said. "I had a vision. Jax was abducted by a man. That's all I know."

"Not much to go on," he chided her. "Can't your vision be a little more specific?"

"We know who has her," I finally spat out. I was getting frustrated by the lack of urgency that Detective Whitman and the other officer had shown us. "It's the same guy who killed Morgan."

"So you know who killed Morgan?" he asked in surprise.

We all nodded.

"I'm all ears," he said, leaning back in his chair.

"Well, after Jax went missing and Holly had her vision that she was stolen, we went downstairs to try and find Sorceress –er, Miss Stone, to report Jax missing, but we had no idea where to look for her. It was late, about midnight and we were in the Winston Hall lobby, and we saw a suspicious figure walk past the courtyard window. So Alba and I snuck outside and followed the figure into a graveyard," I rambled.

"A graveyard," he repeated.

"Yeah, did you know that our campus had a graveyard on site?" I asked him.

He shook his head. "I don't think that I did," he admitted.

"Well, it does. And we followed this suspicious character to this graveyard. He was performing some type of ritual, but it was in a different language, so I don't know what kind of spell it was. There was a light show and wind and chanting, and well, it was super creepy," I said and then took a deep breath.

"Ok, then what?" I was shocked that he didn't seem surprised about the light show and the chanting. I guess Libby and Cinder were right. This town was used to paranormal things happening on a frequent basis.

"Ok, so then he stopped chanting, and he picked up a shovel and a tarp and put them inside this, like, garden shed that was in the middle of the cemetery."

"Did you get a good look at him?" the detective asked.

I nodded. "I know *exactly* who it was. I did a little digging on the internet and found out that the man Alba and I saw tonight is Morgan Hartford's *uncle*, Seymour Hartford. He's the custodian at The Institute," I revealed.

"Seymour Hartford?" Detective Whitman looked at us skeptically.

We all nodded.

"You think Seymour Hartford killed his niece?"

We all nodded again. We were beginning to look like a dashboard full of bobbleheads by this point.

"You can't be serious. Why would Seymour Hartford kill his brother's only daughter?"

I leaned forward, splaying my hands out in front of me. "What? You want us to do *everything* for you? Want me to go out and apprehend him for you too?" I asked sarcastically.

"Well, typically when you accuse someone of murder

you have a reasonable idea of a motive for the crime," he said, ignoring my sarcasm.

"I just told you that he was in the cemetery of our school, at midnight, performing a magical ritual with a shovel and a tarp and that he's related to a girl that just died and another girl from the school where he works disappeared in the same night. For crying out loud, do you need me to draw you a map to Morgan's body for you to believe me?"

"It *would* be nice to have her body back, as a matter of fact," the detective said with a little chuckle.

"You think this is *funny*?" Alba asked with flaring nostrils. Her temper had finally been ignited. "Our friend is missing, and you think we're playing games here?"

"Settle down. I know this is serious stuff. But you have no proof that your friend has been abducted and only some weird happenings around The Institute. That doesn't exactly constitute a murder. And on top of that, you're accusing Roger Hartford's brother of murdering his niece. I find it highly improbable that Morgan's uncle would want to kill her."

"Isn't it true, Detective, that most violent crimes are committed by people that the victim knew?" Sweets asked.

Detective Whitman looked down. "Yeah, that's true."

"And you don't have Morgan's body, and Seymour Hartford was seen with a shovel and a tarp. He was also seen performing a spell. What else do you need to know? This needs to be investigated."

"Ok, fine. I'll investigate Seymour Hartford,"

Detective Whitman promised. "Are we done here?" He stood up to leave, slamming the file shut as if that were it.

"What about my roommate?" I demanded.

"Call me when she's been missing for 24 hours." He started towards the door.

Holly stood up and put her hands on her hips angrily. "But she could be dead in 24 hours!"

"I'm sorry girls. She was last seen walking away on her own. You have no evidence that she's been taken. When she's been gone for 24 hours, then I can do something about it. Until then, I'm sorry, my hands are tied."

"So what are we supposed to do?" Alba demanded.

"Might I suggest alerting Miss Stone. She has an obligation to know the whereabouts of her students. If one is missing, I'm sure she can perform a campus-wide search. I'd start there."

"But we don't know how to get a hold of her before morning. It's late. I have no idea where her room is, and I don't have her number," I complained.

"How about this, I'll let Miss Stone know about your concerns for your roommate. Now, if you don't mind, ladies, I need to go home and catch a few winks before I start that investigation on Seymour Hartford." He held a hand out and waited for the four of us to file out of the office. "Officer Vargas here will let you out. Good night."

The officer who had let us in buzzed us out and we spilled out onto the quiet street in front of the police station.

"What do we do now?" Sweets asked sadly.

I shrugged. "We go back to campus. In the morning, we're going back to that cemetery, and we're going to find Jax and hopefully, Morgan's body!"

CHAPTER FOURTEEN

It hadn't occurred to us that Detective Whitman would call Sorceress Stone before he went home that morning. I guess we assumed since he hadn't taken us seriously, he would have waited until a more reasonable hour to alert her to our concerns, but boy were we ever wrong. We entered Winston Hall a little over 2 o'clock in the morning, exhausted and worried about our friend. We had agreed on the drive home that we'd all get a couple of hours sleep and wake up at the crack of dawn and begin our search for Jax. We hadn't expected to be confronted by Sorceress Stone the minute we walked n.

She was waiting for us in the lobby, wearing what I could only assume were her witch pajamas – flowy white full-length garb, tied loosely around her waist. Her hair was shockingly unkempt and flared out around her head like she'd just poked her finger into an electrical socket.

Daytime Sorceress Stone scared me most of the time, but nighttime Sorceress Stone was almost even *more* intimidating, if that were possible.

"Do you girls not have a brain in your collective bodies?" she raged at us. "What did I tell you about going to the police?"

Sweets and Holly hung their heads, but Alba and I challenged her anger. "We were trying to save our friend!" I hollered back at her.

"You should have woken me!" she snapped.

"We wanted to, but we don't know where your room is and there was no one down here to talk to! How were we supposed to get a hold of you?" Alba demanded.

"There's a phone on the wall over there, you simply pick it up and dial 666," she instructed, thumping the side of her head as if it were the simplest thing in the world and anyone should know.

We looked to where she had pointed. Indeed, there was a small phone attached to the wall. "How were we supposed to know that that was there?" I asked her petulantly.

"Did you even *read* the emergency material that we put in your registration packet?" she asked.

The four of us looked at each other, defeated. No one had apparently read that. I bet Jax had read it.

"Oh, you didn't, did you," she chastised patronizingly. "If you had, you'd see what to do in an emergency situation. The first thing it says to do is to *call Sorceress Stone*. It *most certainly* does not say to call the Aspen Falls Police Department."

"We didn't know, and my roommate has been abducted," I said, this time a little more quietly. The wind had sort of left my sails with the revelation that there indeed had been a way to contact her.

"Your roommate has been abducted. Who is your roommate again?" she asked me.

"Jax," I told her.

Her eyes grew large. "Jax has been abducted? You saw her get abducted?"

Our heads shook.

"I had a vision, Sorceress Stone," Holly told her.

"What was your vision?" she demanded.

"That someone grabbed her. It was a man. I couldn't see his face. And she's being held in a room. Her hands are bound, and her mouth is covered with tape."

"How long ago did this happen?"

"She wandered off about eight last night. We haven't seen her since," I said.

"I can't believe you're just now reporting this. I've had it with the four of you," she stormed. "Follow me, now." She took off up the stairs towards our rooms, gliding up the stairs as if she were floating. We followed her past the second floor, where our rooms were and up higher and higher. As we walked, I wondered if she were taking us to a magical room where she'd teach us how to do a spell to figure out how to get Jax back or to see where she was. Higher and higher we climbed until we were at the top of the building. She took a small key ring from her waist and quietly unlocked the room and led us inside.

"What's this room?" Alba asked as the four of us girls peered out the window to see our view from that high up. Unfortunately, it was too dark to see anything except the glow of the moon and the way the moon reflected off of the tops of the trees.

Sorceress Stone moved back towards the doorway. "This, girls, is what I like to call, Purgatory."

I looked at her in astonishment. "Purgatory?"

She looked down her long thin nose at us. "Your punishment. You'll stay here until I see fit to let you out. Maybe then you'll learn your lesson. You come to me, not the police when something happens. I've warned you. Now let this be your lesson." With that and before we could fight her, she slammed the door on us, and we heard a key turn in the lock.

I pulled on the door handle. It didn't budge. "You can't do this to us!" I hollered, pounding on the heavy wooden door.

Sweets began to wring her hands, "Did she just lock us in here?"

"It'll be alright, Sweets. We'll get out of here," I assured her.

"Step back everyone, I'm going to try and open the door," Alba commanded.

Sweets, Holly and I got behind Alba. She stood up straight, shaking her body, she tried to release the tension from her shoulders and unclutter her mind. She closed her eyes and concentrated on the solid arched door.

We watched her in her state of concentration. We could see the energy beginning to build inside of her. She lifted her arms and flattened her hands, aiming her palms at the door. Finally, she unleashed the energy burst towards the door and opened her eyes.

I watched, as did the rest of the girls, as the energy bubble Alba had unleashed burst against the door.

"This room is insulated against magical powers," Alba said in frustration.

"How do you know?" Sweets asked.

"My mom ended up doing it to our whole house. When I'd escaped one too many times, she insulated it. My telekinesis is ineffective in an insulated environment," she sighed and fell onto a chair.

"You're saying we're stuck?" Holly asked, looking around. "What if we need to use a bathroom?"

"There's a door over there. Maybe it's a bathroom," I suggested.

Holly walked across the large open room and poked her head through the door. "Yeah, it's a bathroom."

"Great," Alba said, rolling her eyes.

"Isn't this illegal?" I asked.

"We're in *witch school*. Who you gonna call?" Alba asked smarmily.

Holly and Sweets looked at each other with a little smile. "Ghostbusters!" they answered in unison.

I rolled my eyes. "Not the time for humor, ladies. We're stuck in here, what are we supposed to do about Jax? What if Stone doesn't let us out until it's too late? We've got to think of something!"

Holly yawned and looked at the two sets of bunk beds in the back of the room. "Ok, I'll think of something, in the morning. I've got to get my beauty rest, ladies."

Sweets nodded. "Me too, I'm exhausted. I just hope we get breakfast in the morning. I'm already starving."

I looked at Alba. "We should get some shut eye too, Alba. We'll be useless tomorrow to find Jax if we don't get some sleep. And there's nothing we can do right now, anyway. Maybe in the daylight we'll figure out a way to escape."

"Agreed. Alright girls, take a bunk. We'll figure this all out in the morning."

CHAPTER FIFTEEN

Sitting in the uppermost room of Winston Hall the next morning was quite the drag. I thought *classes* were snoresville, but this was the worst. Not only were the beds probably the lumpiest in the entire place, but the company was a drag.

At the very least, Sweets was usually tolerable, and Holly came in at a dull second, but locked away with no food or drink wore on Sweets quickly. She went from, well, Sweet, to sour by lunchtime.

"Why won't she bring us any food?" she demanded.

"We're being punished, Sweets," Alba snarled. She'd always been a grouchy person, but throw three sour girls on top of Alba and shake, and craziness ensued.

"I realize we're being punished, but this is ridiculous. I don't even think she can do this. It's like corporal punishment!"

I rolled my eyes. I'd heard it all morning.

"And I'm pretty sure I'm hypoglycemic," Sweets continued. "If I don't eat, I'll probably pass out. And then what? We don't even have any way to call for an ambulance."

"Not that we're allowed to call an ambulance anyway," I added.

"Exactly, this is crazy. I can't believe my mother wanted me to go to this school. If she knew the kind of conditions I'm being subjected to, she'd have me out of here in a jiffy," Sweets continued.

I looked around despondently. "Well then, maybe you should call her," I suggested.

"I will call her! I promise, when we get out of here, I'm calling her."

My gaze traveled out the window as I sat in the window seat in the north facing window. The colors of the trees from up here were simply amazing. Fall had truly settled into Aspen Falls. I was able to see the cemetery behind the campus from our height. Beyond the cemetery and up the hill was another castle with two tall turrets that soared high into the sky, taller than the trees around it.

Just then we heard the door latch unlock and the door opened with a loud creak. Libby and Cinder walked in, each with two trays of food in their arms.

"Well, well, well," Alba said as she walked towards them. "What do we have here?"

"Lunch time, ladies," Cinder sang as Sweets immediately came to claim a tray of food.

"Well, it's about time!" she yelled.

"Sorry, we had to wait for the cafeteria to make it," Libby said handing her two trays to Alba and me.

I looked at the open door. "Hey ladies, we've got an open door," I pointed out.

Cinder shook her head. "Don't do it, Mercy. I know you want to. I know Stone locking you in here is the pits, but we've all been in purgatory at one time or another. She's hard on freshman, but she lightens up. Trust me."

"When is she planning on our punishment being over?" Holly asked.

"I heard her telling Hobbs that she'd let you out sometime after lunch was over," Libby told us.

I looked at Libby curiously. "Did you hear that Jax is missing?"

Libby nodded her head. "Yeah, it's all over school."

Sweets stopped eating. "So she hasn't come back yet?"

Cinder shook her head sadly. "No."

"Is anyone doing anything to try and find her?" Alba asked angrily.

"I'm really not sure," Libby said.

"Hey Cinder," I said, waving her towards me in the window seat. "Come here, would you?"

The red-head walked towards me, and I pointed to the castle across the valley. "Is that The Black Witch's castle?"

Cinder nodded. "Yeah, why?"

"Is there any way she's got anything to do with all of this?"

"You think she did this?" Cinder asked.

"I think Seymour is behind all of this," I told her honestly. "But I feel like he could have a partner. Maybe he's working for The Black Witch."

"The police investigated Seymour. It's all over school. They searched the cemetery and his place. They didn't find anything," said Libby.

"And he had an alibi," Cinder added. "He was at work that morning. He's got a timecard to prove it. There's no way he had time to kill Morgan."

My heart dropped. I was so sure it was him. "You're kidding. They couldn't find Jax?"

She shook her head. "Uh-uh. No sign of her."

"Did you hear? We found him doing magic in the cemetery late last night. Did you know he was a wizard?" I asked the older girls.

Cinder nodded. "Yeah, we all knew that. He's a wizard, but he's not a bad guy. He's grumpy and all, but he's not a bad guy. I really don't think he would have hurt his niece."

"He's so creepy, though! And Morgan's dad really set off my senses," I added. "I was sure there was something going on with those two."

Libby stood up. "We have to get going. We really weren't even supposed to be talking to you four."

Cinder nodded. "Yeah, Stone is probably going to give us hell for it. So if she asks, we dropped off your food and didn't say a thing!"

I smiled. "Got it. Thanks for the food and the intel."

"No problem," Libby said. "We'll see you two later.

Libby and Cinder left, locking the door behind them as they went.

"We should have just left," Alba sighed.

"Why didn't you, the door was open?" Holly asked her.

Alba sat down and picked at her food. "Because I need this school. And because I was hungry."

The four of us devoured our food quickly, and it gave all of us a sudden burst of energy. We investigated our holding cell and found that in the back of the closet was a hidden staircase that took us to the top of the turret we were in. Holly and Sweets had no interest in exploring, so Alba and I took the stairs all the way up to the very top of the castle.

"Wow, it's cool up here," I hollered down the stairs to Holly and Sweets. My voice echoed against the stone walls and down the stairs.

"Look, Red, this must be where they store their old stuff. Check this out," Alba said and led me over to an adjoining room. It was filled with old pieces of furniture and trunks of old clothes. Alba opened a trunk and pulled out an old gown.

"Cool. This would be fun to spend a day going through," I said to her.

"Well, we've got a day."

"Really? Do you want to go through all of this today?" I asked in surprise. That was the last thing that I felt like doing.

"Fine, oh, look at this, a box of old books!" Alba said with interest.

"Spell books?" I asked.

She shook her head. "Nah, I don't think so. This one looks like a yearbook!"

I joined her and pulled a book out of the box too. "This one is a yearbook too," I said, blowing dust off of the leather bound cover. "The Paranormal Institute, 1936," I read.

"They had yearbooks back then? Crazy!" Alba said.

I flipped the book open and looked through a few of the pages. I recognized many of the areas of campus in the book. "Oh look, there's the Canterbury Building," I said and showed Alba the picture.

"Cool," she said.

We heard a voice float from the downstairs to the attic. "Find anything good up there?" Holly hollered.

"Yeah, we'll take some stuff down," I hollered back. "Come on, let's take a few of these down, the girls are going to love these. It'll give us a way to pass the time before Stone decides to let us out."

Alba and I put everything away except two yearbooks. We climbed back down the stairs and spent the next hour pouring over the yearbooks. The fashion back then was so different. The ladies in their fancy dresses looked so properly witchy that I felt like I really didn't deserve the title.

"Look at this one, is this *Stone?*" Alba asked, pointing to a thin young woman in a long black dress holding onto the arm of a handsome man in a suit. Her hair was dark, though, and it didn't quite look like Stone.

"It looks like her, except the hair. What's the caption

say?" I said, pushing my glasses up on the bridge of my nose.

Alba held the book closer to her face. "It says *BethAnn and Oliver enjoy the Autumnal Equinox celebration in the town square*."

"Huh, not Stone, that's weird. Totally thought it looked like her," I said. "Maybe it's her mother or something."

Just then we heard the door click and it flew open with force. I quickly grabbed the book from Alba and slammed it shut, shoving it into the back of my pants, covering it up with my top.

"Well, have you girls learned your lesson yet?" Sorceress Stone asked from the doorway.

We all nodded like zombie robots. Of course, we'd say we'd learned our lesson. We needed to get out of their so we could go hunt down Jax.

"What have you learned?" she asked exasperatedly.

No one said anything. So she pointed her little bony finger at Holly. "You, what did you learn?"

"Don't call the cops, call you if there is an emergency," Holly said in a robotic voice.

"Good. Now, about Seymour Hartford. The police have conducted an investigation on Seymour. He has an airtight alibi for the morning of the murder. He was working on campus, and he has several witnesses that will swear to that fact."

"What about Jax?" I demanded.

A dark shadow seemed to cross in front of Sorceress Stone's eyes. "We're working on finding her. You need to stay out of it."

"She's my roommate, how can I just stay out of it?" I asked despondently.

"And she's *our* friend," Holly added.

"Listen, ladies, I can appreciate you wanting to help your friend. But we do things a certain way around here. We will find her. Stay out of it," she ordered. "Now, your punishment is complete. You may go."

With that, the four of us grabbed the few things we'd had with us when we got to the room and scampered out of the prison and back to my dorm room. Sneaks ran to me almost immediately and wrapped himself around my leg, purring on contact. I'd forgotten that I'd left him in my room. "Hey buddy," I said as I reached down and scratched under his chin. "Did you miss me?" If I hadn't been so worried about Jax, I might have given more thought to the fact that it looked like he nodded his head after my rhetorical question.

Before spinning on my heel to look at the girls, I took the yearbook out of the back of my shirt and threw it down on the bed. "Now what? Where do we start?"

"I'll tell you where we start," Alba said. She grabbed the Aspen Falls snow globe off of Jax's desk and tossed it to Holly. "We're going to start with Holly. Jax needs you to see her again."

Holly nodded and took a seat on Jax's desk chair. She closed her eyes and took a deep breath, then put the snow globe between both of her hands and exhaled while focusing her energy on the item. We could tell it was working again when her body went rigid as it had the last time she'd had a vision. This time her trance lasted almost a minute, causing her to crumple forward when she was finally released from its hold.

"Holly!" Sweets hollered and took a step forward to block her from falling to the floor.

"Holly, you saw something, right?" I asked her.

Holly nodded her head but was so weak that she could barely speak.

"Get her juice," I commanded Alba who was standing behind me.

Alba surprisingly obeyed my command without snipping back at me and got Holly a bottle of juice from our tiny fridge. "Here."

I opened it for Holly and put it to her lips, helping her to drink it. "You alright?"

She took a deep breath after her drink and sat back, resting for a few long moments. "Saw Jax," she was able to manage to croak out cryptically.

"You did? Good, is she alright?" I asked immediately.

We all watched her closely; waiting for any sign that she was still alive. Holly managed to nod. "Alive."

Alba, Sweets and I let out a whoop and holler, excited to hear that our friend was still alive. Holly reached out and grabbed my hand. "Jax. In trouble."

CHAPTER SIXTEEN

I took a deep breath and nodded. We all knew she was in trouble. We could only hope for the best and cross our fingers that she wasn't in immediate trouble.

"Sleep," Holly murmured with her eyes lids slowly getting heavier and heavier. The reading had worn her out, and it was obvious she would need rest before we could continue. We helped her to my bed and Sweets covered her up with the quilt my granny had sewn for me.

I sat down on the floor next to my bed, crossing my legs in front of me like a pretzel. Sneaks immediately jumped off the bed and curled up in a ball inside of the little nest I had created.

I scratched the top of his head and behind his ears, and he looked up at me earnestly. "Meow," he said as if telling me that felt good.

"Oh, does that feel good?" I asked him as I scratched

his other ear.

He nodded. This time, the fact that he nodded in response to a question registered in my brain. "Guys, I swear, Sneaks just nodded at me."

"Dude, he's a cat," Alba said, dismissing me immediately.

"But he *nodded* at me."

Sweets patted my head. "I think you need some sugar, Mercy."

I swatted her hand away. "Sweets, everything in life can't be resolved with snacks." I looked at Sneaks more intently this time and rubbed his chin. He closed his eyes as I scratched. "Do you like to have your chin scratched, Sneaks?"

This time Sneaks opened his eyes. Looked me clearly in the eye and with a pleasant expression on his face, he nodded his head pleasantly.

My eyes nearly shot out of my skull.

Alba shot out of her seat and towards the door. "Dude! The cat totally just nodded his head at you!"

"That was crazy!" said Sweets excitedly.

"I told you!"

"Yeah, but this time I *saw* him do it. Ask him another question," Alba suggested. Her nerves were jittery.

"What should I ask him?" I asked, perplexed. "He's a *cat.*"

"I don't know!" Alba countered.

"Here, ask him if he wants a snack," Sweets suggested and offered me a fish cracker from the box on Jax's desk.

"Seriously? You think he wants a fish cracker? You

realize it's not made of fish, right?" I said with a chuckle.

Sweets nodded. "Of course, silly. Ask him anyway."

I rolled my eyes and looked at Sneaks who was sitting up attentively, actively listening to our conversation. "Sneaks, do you want a snack?" I asked and handed him the fish cracker.

This time he shook his head from side to side *and* lifted one soft furry paw to touch my hand and gently push it away.

"Oh my god," Alba's eyes were huge. "He can totally understand you."

"This is so bizarre," I said with a huge smile. "I wish I could understand him."

"You're taking Animal Spirits class aren't you?" Sweets asked me.

I nodded weakly. "Yeah, but it's only been a week. We haven't gotten to familiars yet."

"You have your spell book from class, though, right?" Sweets asked.

"Yeah."

"Ok, there should be a spell in there somewhere that could help us out. Where's your book?"

I pulled my backpack out from the side of my desk and unzipped it, pulling out the thick Animal book. I handed it to Sweets and watched Sneaks as she flipped through the pages. His soft furry face seemed to watch the three of us intently as if he were waiting patiently for us to find a spell.

"Wouldn't it be crazy if all this time Sneaks was able to understand me?" I asked Alba.

"Crazy is putting it mildly," she said.

"Animal protection spells, animal love spells, animal transformation spells," she read off as she flipped through the pages. "Here it is. I found it! Animal familiar spells!" Sweets said and shoved the book in my lap. "We need three black candles, three hairs from your head and three hairs from Sneaks' head and a crystal bowl."

"Jax might have the candles, look in her cupboard," I instructed Alba to look in the cabinet behind her.

"I've got a crystal serving bowl in my room!" Sweets declared. "I'll run and get it."

Sweets left the room while Alba and I searched through Jax's cabinet for her candle collection. Tucked away in the back of the cabinet, inside a little plastic tote, was an assortment of candles that I had seen her drag out earlier in the week while she was doing her homework.

"Awesome, she's got black ones," I said and plucked three short votives from the tote.

Sweets came back, having quickly changed out of her bathrobe and slippers into a more appropriate pair of leggings and a long t-shirt, with a small smudge of pink frosting visible just above the right side of her lip. She brought with her a small round crystal serving bowl.

"I won't even ask *why* you have pink frosting on your lip," I said with a laugh.

"Fair enough," she said with a nod. "Now, the book says we light the candles and pour the wax drops into the crystal bowl. We let the wax firm just a smidge and press the hairs of yours and the hairs of Sneaks together into the wax all the while chanting the spell in the book. Then you transfer your energy to him and bam! Talking cat!"

Alba quickly lit the candles and set them each one by one onto Jax's desk.

"Sounds easy enough," I said with a big smile. I looked at Sneaks with a crooked grin. "You up for this buddy?"

Amazingly Sneaks nodded again, and I actually thought I saw him smile.

"This is so amazing," I said as Alba plucked three auburn colored hairs from my head and Sweets plucked three black hairs from Sneaks'.

Carefully Alba dropped the melted wax into the bowl from each of the three candles, and as they began to firm up, I gingerly pressed our hairs together into the wax. Focusing my energy as I'd been taught in class, I concentrated on Sneaks and his aura.

"Spirits above I summon thee, bless me with this familiar cat bound to me. Spirits above I summon thee, bless me with this familiar cat bound to me. Spirits above I summon thee, bless me with this familiar cat bound to me." Over and over I repeated the chant until I could feel the energy building inside of my body. Inhaling one more deep breath, I said the chant one more time. "Spirits above I summon thee, bless me with this familiar cat bound to me!" Then I exhaled blowing the energy from my body towards Sneaks.

I opened my eyes and looked at the cat. He was sitting upright with his eyes closed. He appeared to be trying to absorb my energy.

"Sneaks? You ok, little guy?" I asked him nervously.

Quietly he opened his eyes and looked at me. "We should start this off right, I'm not a little guy, Mercy, I'm a female cat. You've been calling me little guy all week, and it's been driving me bananas!" Sneaks said casually while Sweets, Alba and I stared.

"MOM?!" I asked, my eyes huge. The voice was unmistakable; it was my *mother's voice!*

"Yes Mercy Bear, it's Mom."

"Mother! I told you to stop calling me that. How in the heck are you inside of Sneaks?" I demanded, peering closely at the cat.

Sneaks sort of tilted his head to the side and appeared to shrug at me. "Eh, it's a spell. No big deal."

"No big deal, this is *crazy!*" I told her animatedly.

"Took you long enough to figure out I was trying to talk to you," she quipped. "I've literally been trying to communicate with you *all week.*"

"I had no idea! Are you trying to *spy* on me or something?"

"Not originally. I just wanted to be able to see you and talk to you, you know, while you're away."

"Hello? Ever heard of *Skype?*" I asked.

"Yeah, I have. Consider this *Skype.* For witches. We could call it Skitches. Or Wype. I think I like Skitches better now that I hear it out loud."

"Mother! Focus!"

"Right, sorry, sorry. Anyway, I hadn't meant to be hanging around so much, but with this Hartford girl murder and now with Jax missing, I've just been so worried about you girls."

I looked back at Alba and Sweets who were standing back quietly watching me interact with my cat. "Can you understand them too?" I asked my mother.

"Yes, I can understand all witches. Except Jax, for some reason I couldn't understand Jax," she added.

I nodded my head sadly. "It's because Jax isn't a witch, Mom. She's been pretending."

"Pretending to be a witch? Whatever for?"

"Long story, but the shortened version is - she just wanted to be a witch."

"Now I understand why she's been overcompensating with all the overdone witch apparel."

"Yeah," I agreed. Then I turned to look at the girls. "Can you guys hear her?"

They both shook their heads.

"Nope, but I can see Sneaks' mouth moving, just cat noises come out, though," Alba said. "And obviously we can hear *your* end of the conversation."

"Ditto," Sweets agreed. "Oh. My. GOSH. It worked!" she cheered excitedly. "It worked! It worked! It worked, it worked, it worked!" She danced around the room.

"This is so bizarre," I said with a little chuckle. "I never thought I'd be able to communicate with an animal."

"You're doing really well, Merc. I'm impressed. Your powers must be growing already. That's what happens when a witch becomes a woman. It happens very quickly. Wait until you turn 20. You'll have your full powers by then. I'm thankful you're in a place that will teach you to focus your powers on good, not evil."

"Mom, I'm worried about Jax. I don't know what to do," I told her honestly.

"Having Holly do a reading is a smart idea, but sweetheart, I'm worried about you and your friends. You must be extremely careful. All of your lives are in danger. I've been getting strong readings all week," Mom told me anxiously. "

"Ok, Mom. We'll be careful. I don't suppose you saw who took Jax did you?"

"I wish I had, but I didn't see anything."

"Ok, as soon as Holly wakes up, we're going to figure this out. But you can't stay here Mom. We aren't allowed to have pets, and we're already on very thin ice with Sorceress Stone."

"I understand, leave the window open. I'll go for now, maybe I can do some digging around campus and see what I can find out," she added and hopped up onto the windowsill.

"Ok, thanks, Mom." I gave her a little smile, and suddenly I realized that I'd missed her badly over the past week. I wished she were standing in front of me so I could give her a big hug and tell her how much I loved her. Realizing I had the next best thing in front of me, I took a step forward and gave Sneaks a hug and whispered in her ear, "Love you, Mom." Then I opened my dorm window.

She whispered back, "Love you too, Mercy Bear. Be safe." Then Sneaks jumped out the window and across to the fire escape next door.

"That. Was. AMAZING," Sweets hollered as soon as

Sneaks was out the window.

"So it was *your mom* this whole time?" Alba asked. She was astounded as I was.

"Yeah and she said she's been getting strong readings this week and that we need to be careful, our lives are in danger," I repeated what my mother had told me to the girls.

"Our lives are in *danger*?" Sweets asked, biting her fingernails nervously. "Did she say anything about Jax's life?"

"It's in danger too," said a voice from behind us.

We turned around to find Holly sitting up on the edge of my bed. She had a hand to her head and was rubbing it with squinted eyes.

"Holly!" Sweets cheered.

"You alright? You don't look so great," I told her as I knelt down next to her on the floor.

"Ugh, I feel like I have a hangover," she admitted. "I didn't feel this bad last time I did a reading."

"Two in one day must be too much," said Alba.

She put her arms out for us to take. "Help me up? I want to go sit in a chair."

Alba and I each took an arm and helped her to the desk chair she had sat in earlier. Once she was seated comfortably, we all stared down at her.

She looked up, her eyes panned across our faces nervously. "Gosh, I feel like I'm being interrogated!"

"We've just been waiting anxiously for you to come to so we could find out what you saw!"

"I saw Jax," she began slowly. "She was lying on a

hard, cold surface. Like a stone altar or something. Her hands were bound by her side. Her legs were bound to the table. Her mouth was taped shut." Holly's body shuddered as tears began to fall down her cheeks.

Sweets, who also had tears in her eyes to hear of Jax's predicament, wrapped her arms around Holly's neck.

"Oh, girls, it was so horrible to see her like that." Holly's body shook as she talked.

My heart immediately sank. "This is all my fault. I feel terrible that I was so bad to Jax. If it hadn't been for me, she'd be safe and sound right now."

"You don't know that," Sweets said quietly, though I knew what she was thinking. I knew what all of them were thinking. I was right. It was my fault. I had to do whatever it took to find Jax and bring her back safely.

"What else did you see Holly?" Alba asked her.

"It's kind of fuzzy, like an old black and white TV with lots of static. I know I saw candles flickering on the walls in the room, it felt like she were being prepped for a ritual or an offering or a spell or something. I'm not really sure."

"Could you see anyone?" I asked.

Holly shook her head, "No. I didn't see any faces, but I could see someone in the corner working at a table. He…he…he had on a ring! I remember now! I recognized the ring! It was the boy I met at the social last night. Evan! It was Evan's ring!"

Alba and I looked at each other. Finally a break in the case! Jax was at the boys' camp. Finally, we had a place to focus our energies on. "We need to go." I glanced down at Holly. "Are you going to be ok? Maybe you should stay here. We can help you to your dorm, and you can lie down for awhile."

Holly stood up energetically. "No, I'm fine. I'm going to help you find Jax and bring her back!"

CHAPTER SEVENTEEN

The sun was shining brightly in the courtyard when we burst out of the Winston Hall glass doors on a mission. The air smelled fresh and new as if it had rained in the night. We started towards Warner Hall, the men's dormitory, when Sweets grabbed my arm and stopped me on the outskirts of the courtyard barrier.

"Are we just going to walk in there with no plan?" she asked nervously. "I'm not even sure if girls are *allowed* in the wizard's dormitory."

"Houston let me inside last night," I said.

"Who is Houston?" Alba asked in confusion.

"Oh, you missed a lot of last night. He's a cowboy wizard I met."

"A cowboy wizard?" She looked perplexed.

"He's a wizard from Texas and he wears a cowboy hat and boots. I know – kind of weird," I said.

"But he's *super* hot," Sweets chimed in.

I couldn't deny her accusation. He was super hot. "Anyway, I was allowed in. If we get stopped, I'll say I lost my bracelet last night or something."

"Ok, so we go in. How will we know where to go?" Holly asked.

"Intuition," I said and tapped a finger against my temple.

"Seriously? This whole operation is based on *your* intuition?" Holly seemed skeptical.

"The closer we get to Jax, the better my senses will be. It's like playing the hot/cold game. I promise. If we get close to her, I'll know it."

"Fine, let's go," Holly agreed.

We crossed through the low stone wall surrounding the courtyard and the sign that read Warner Hall, Paranormal Institute for Wizards, Men's Dormitory. Several men were milling around in the lobby as we entered, and quite rightly so, we found ourselves the objects of quite a bit of speculation. Just like we never saw guys on our side, they likely never saw women on theirs.

"Hello," I said, nodding at the first curious onlooker that looked like he might approach us and ask us what we were doing in their building. He nodded back and we kept walking.

Nothing seemed to spark my senses, so we just began walking towards a set of stairs next to their lounge area. A tall man wearing a long robe approached us. His hands were buried in the sleeves of his robe, and he bowed over them as a greeting to us. "May I help you find something ladies?"

"Oh, no, thank you," I said politely, hoping that he would just go away.

"Our dormitories are up this way, we don't allow women up there unless they are escorted by one of our students. Are you here to see someone in particular?" he asked, looking down his long thin nose at us, reminding me almost immediately of Sorceress Stone.

"Yes, uh – we are," I said without thinking. "Houston. Houston Brooks. I met him last night at the social, and oooh-ee, did I fall for that man," I quipped. My natural instinct to lie in a sticky situation returned without a second thought.

"Aww, how sweet of you to say," I heard a man's voice say from behind me. "Here I thought you didn't like me much."

My cheeks immediately pinched up into my eyes as I winced. *Ugh, of course he was down here.* "Hello, Hugh," I said turning around to face the ruggedly handsome cowboy.

"Hello Mercy," he nodded at me. His broad smile and twinkling eyes made me want to vomit all over his polished leather boots.

"I'm sure flattered that you wanted to come see me today. And I see that you brought a few of your friends. Ladies," he added and then tipped his cowboy hat to my friends. Why did he have to be so darn adorable?

"Hugh, dear," I purred, linking arms with him. I gave the dorm room attendant a giggly smile. I prided myself on being quite the little actress when I needed to be. "The girls and I really need to speak to you, is there any way we could speak in private. Say in your room?"

The man who had stopped us at the bottom of the stairs looked at us girls suspiciously.

"Umm, well, I have class in…" Hugh looked down at his watch. "Five minutes."

"Oh, it will only take a second," Holly assured him as she twirled a long blonde lock with her finger.

"Ok, then, sure, my room's up here," Hugh said and smiled at the gatekeeper who gave us a little nod and then disappeared down a corridor.

Taking obvious joy in my little theatrics, Hugh kept hold of my arm while we walked up the stairs. I fumed while we walked, angry at myself for resorting to *flirting* to get upstairs. I never flirted. I wasn't a flirt. I guessed that Holly's charms were starting to rub off on me or something.

"In here," he said and unlocked his room. We all filed in. His room was much less frou-frou than mine was. He had a set of bunk beds with navy blue bedding, and his desk had a little fan on it with some books and pencils scattered about. No carpet. No posters. No mini fridge or flat screen television.

"Who's your decorator?" I asked with a little smile as I leaned up against his desk.

He looked around. "You don't like my decorating skills?"

"No, no. I like it. Very, um, minimalistic," I said.

Houston threw his backpack down on his bed and then sat on the top of his desk and looked me up and down with an adorable little smirk. "So, did I leave that big of an impression on you Mercy? You had to come and see me?"

"Yeah, that's what this is all about," I said dryly. "I just – couldn't stay away."

"You've been all she's talked about since last night," Alba added with twinkling eyes.

Houston looked me in the eyes, "Isn't *that* interesting. I'm flattered."

I couldn't take it anymore. I rolled my eyes and shot Alba a menacing glance. "Oh, don't be flattered. We aren't here for you."

Houston did his best to look wounded. "You're not?" he grasped at his heart as he fell backwards on the desk.

"Oh stop. We're here about our friend," I said.

"You're friend? You mean the one that Freddy got frisky with last night? Look…I'm nothing like that, I swear," Houston said and put his hands up as if to say he surrendered. "I tried to tell you, but you ran off."

"He's your friend, isn't he?" I asked.

"I just met the guy this week! He's actually my buddy Carl's roommate. I don't even really know Freddy. Friday night was the first night we hung out."

"Do you happen to know Evan?" Holly interjected when she realized I wasn't getting to the point quickly enough.

"Evan Lancaster?"

Holly shrugged. "Are there two Evan's here?"

"I have no idea. The only Evan I know is Evan Lancaster. He's a second year."

"Stocky guy with a pinky ring?" Holly asked.

Houston nodded. "Yeah. That's him."

"Do you know where he lives?" Alba asked.

"I don't know his room number or anything, but I'm sure he's in this building." He narrowed his eyes and peered at the four of us. "Why, what's going on? What does this have to do with your friend?" Unless Houston was a really good liar, it was obvious he had nothing to do with Jax's disappearance. He literally seemed like he was clueless about what was going on.

"Well, she…" Sweets began, but Alba stepped in front of her before she could finish.

"She just has a little thing for him, no big deal," Alba finished. "I suppose we shouldn't hold you up any longer."

He looked at the four of us like we were on drugs and then slowly nodded. "Ooookay," he said slowly. "Yeah, it was really nice chatting?"

"Oh, yeah, us too," I nodded. "See you around."

We let him open the door for us and then waited in the hallway for him to leave first. He gave us an awkward stare once he'd properly locked his door. "After you, ladies," he said and motioned for us to go first.

The four of us held our ground. "Umm, I think we're going to go and try and find Evan, if you don't mind?" I finally said.

"You're not supposed to be up here alone."

"Well, it's really important that we find Evan. I promise we won't pull the fire alarms or toilet paper anybody's room. Trust us?" I asked with the best sweet and innocent face I could muster.

"Hmm. Trust four girls who obviously look like they're up to something?" He watched us closely. "Eh, sure, why not. But if anyone asks, I escorted you outside, and you snuck back in."

I shot him a huge genuine smile. "Got it. Thanks, Hugh," I said.

He smiled back; his perfect teeth glinted white. "You owe me one, Mercy."

"Fine, I owe you one," I agreed.

He turned around to leave and then hollered back down the hallway. "You ladies are my witnesses. Mercy Habernackle owes me one!"

Sweets and Holly giggled as I felt the heat rise to my face. "Now what?" I asked, trying to change gears back to why we were really there.

"We've got to find where Evan's room is. Maybe there's a dorm list somewhere," Holly suggested.

"Do you really think he's got her tied to a stone altar in his *dorm room*?" I asked.

Alba nodded. "Good point. Where else would there be a stone altar?"

Our eyes all lit up. "Basement!" I cried.

"Let's go this way, we can't go back down the main stairs, Grandmaster Flash will stop us," I said.

"Grandmaster Flash?" Alba stared at me with a small smile on her lips while we headed the opposite way down the hall.

I shrugged. "What? I don't know his name. The guy who stopped us at the door that looked like a monk."

Hugh's hallway ended with another set of stone stairs,

which spiraled down to the main floor. At the bottom of the stairs, we peered around and noticed we were at the back of a long corridor.

"This way," I whispered, motioning for the girls to follow me. The hairs on the back of my neck began to move, and I felt tiny tingles along my legs. "We're getting closer. I can feel it."

We moved down the corridor, single file, and kept going until we found another set of stairs at the end of that hallway. Quietly we crept down the stairs and found ourselves in the basement of the boy's dormitory.

"It's dark down here," Sweets whispered nervously.

"Quiet," I hissed. "This way."

We slunk down the hallway, guided by my witchly intuition. Full on goosebumps covered my arms and legs now, and I was beginning to feel the chills coming over me. I knew we were close.

The dank hallway was like a maze of corridors and rooms. I let my feelings guide me and soon enough I was shivering outside of an arched heavy wooden door. "She's in here," I told the girls through chattering teeth. "She's got to be."

"Do we just go in?" Holly asked nervously. "What if Evan is in there?"

"Be prepared to do what you have to do to protect yourself. We've got to save Jax," Alba told us. "Come on."

We pushed up against the heavy door, opening it slowly it creaked loudly. The room was dark, but we could hear a muffled rustling noise coming from inside.

Sweets and Holly clung to my back, and I clung to Alba's, letting her lead the way.

The muffled sound grew louder until finally, through the pitch black, we heard a timid voice call out. "Who's there?"

CHAPTER EIGHTEEN

"Jax?" I whispered to the voice.

"Mercy? Is that you?"

"Yeah, it's Mercy."

"Mercy, oh thank God, yeah, it's Jax. I'm tied down. I can't move," she cried in the darkness.

"We'll get you out of here, Jax," I promised, and the four of us rushed forward blindly.

"Oof," Holly belted out after we heard a loud bang. "Who put that there? Ouch, that hurt."

"Holly? Is that you?"

"Yeah, Jaxie, it's me. Is there a light switch or flashlights or candles or something around here?"

"Holly, on the wall straight ahead of you, there's a desk. Feel around above your head when you get there, there's a pull chain," Jax instructed.

We heard Holly rambling around for a bit and then a

click and the room became dimly illuminated. The room looked like a cross between a torture chamber and a laboratory. The stone walls and dirt floor made the room cold and damp. Chandeliers with candles in them hung from the ceiling, and there were candles in holders on the walls.

Alba snapped her fingers while blowing on the candles in the center of the room and the candles magically lit at once. She did it again, this time aiming her breath at the candles on the wall behind us and lit them easily as well.

"Cool!" Holly cooed excitedly.

Alba smirked at us and shrugged one shoulder, "Party trick."

With the room fully lit we were able to see everything better. Jax was lying on a stone table as Holly had envisioned her earlier. Her arms and legs were bound to the table, and she had a gag tied around her neck that she must have been able to work free.

"Guys, you've got to get me loose, he could be back any minute," she said, her timid voice trembling as she tried to pull her bruised and bloodied wrists free from her leather constraints.

"Jax, take a deep breath, relax," I said, trying to be a calming force. "We're going to get you out of here." Then I turned to Alba who was rifling through a desk across the room. "Find anything to cut these leather straps?"

"I'm looking, I'm looking," she said.

"Guys, what is this?" Sweets said, her voice filled with terror.

I turned around and saw Sweets standing in front of a stainless steel rolling cart with a tarp over it and the outline of a body underneath of it. "Jax?" I asked.

"It's Morgan Hartford," said Jax. The room went deadly silent and the tension increased tenfold.

Alba swung her eyes towards me. "She's got to be here, Mercy."

I nodded and looked around the room. I didn't see anyone else. "Have you seen or heard from her ghost, Jax?"

Jax began to cry. "No! I'm not a witch, remember?"

The realization that Jax had been here all day and night, scared and alone, made me swallow hard. She hadn't even had Morgan's ghost to keep her company. Only Evan and whatever wicked scheme he'd cooked up.

"I'm so sorry, Jax," I said and fell onto her chest. "This is all my fault. If I wasn't so mean to you…"

"It's not your fault Mercy. You didn't know someone was going to do this to me. But we can talk about all of that later. He's going to come back; you have to cut me out of these straps!" She pulled her wrists up as far as they would go and tugged on them as I was sure she'd probably done all night and day.

"Who is going to come back, Jax? Is it Evan?" Holly asked, her eyes filled with fear.

Jax nodded. "Evan and that Freddy."

"Freddy! Freddy had a hand in this?" I asked. "Wait until I get my hands on that creep!"

"He was the one that took me! But Evan is the one that put me down here. I haven't seen Freddy since he passed me over to Evan."

"Do you know what they want with you?" I asked.

"Yeah, I know what Evan wants. He's spent the last five hours trying to do spells to stuff my soul into Morgan's dead body!"

"Stuff your soul into Morgan? For what? How?" Sweets asked.

"Evan said that he found a spell in one of his books that said he could make a mortal come back to life by sacrificing a witch. He was trying to make my spirit come alive in Morgan. But it wouldn't work."

Suddenly, my arms and legs went cold, and I felt an icy shiver run down my back. "Guys, I'm feeling something."

Everyone stopped what they were doing and looked at me.

Nervously, I looked up and scanned the room. I turned around and there she was. Silently in the corner stood a tiny featured blonde girl with a gold cross around her neck.

"Morgan?" I asked.

"You can see me?" Her hand flew nervously to the little cross around her neck as she fingered it lightly.

I smiled at her sadly. "Yeah, I can see you."

"Why can't they see me too?" she asked nervously. "Aren't they witches too?"

"Not all witches are mediums," I shared. "Just some of us are."

"I take it you're talking to Morgan?" Jax asked me.

"Yeah, she's here," I answered.

"Great, well, we can take her with us. But we've got to get out of here!" Jax insisted.

"She's right," Morgan said. "He's a very bad man. If you want your friend to live, you need to get her out of here, now."

"I found a knife, will this work?" Holly asked and held up a scalpel she'd found in one of the desk drawers.

"Yes!" I exclaimed.

"Hurry!" The panic in Jax's voice was real. It sent a shiver of fear through me, making my limbs heavy and slow.

Holly handed the knife to Alba, who promptly began to start slicing at Jax's wristbands.

"I found scissors!" Sweets called out excitedly and went to the cuffs around Jax's ankles and began working at the leather bands.

"You've got to hurry," Jax said again. Her arms and legs bounced on the table as she watched the door. "He's literally going to be back any minute."

"You've got to hold still," Sweets said, holding a hand over her foot to steady it. "I'm going to cut you if you keep kicking like that."

"It's ok Jax, relax. We can take him," Alba assured her.

Jax shook her head. "No, you don't understand. He's a bad bad man. And he's powerful. He's been trying spell after spell on me since I got here."

Alba squatted next to her, working on her wrist cuff. "And look! You're just fine. His spells haven't worked!"

"Only because he thought I was a witch! He still

thinks I'm a witch. He's been trying to do a spell on a witch, not a human. He's not doing them right. If he knew I was just a plain old mortal, he'd know that he was doing them wrong, but I didn't tell him I was just a plain old mortal. He's been freaking out because he can't figure out why his spells aren't working," Jax revealed with a shaky voice. "We have to get Morgan's body out of here too."

Alba freed Jax's right wrist, while Sweets freed one of her legs. Alba walked around the table and began to work on her other wrist while Sweets began to work on the other leg.

"Morgan, can you keep guard in the hallway?" I asked quietly. My heart was thumping in my ears, scared that at any moment we'd have a psychotic wizard to contend with.

She nodded and then disappeared through the wall.

"Jax, I don't think we're going to be able to carry a corpse out of here without someone noticing," I tentatively told her.

"If we leave her body here, he'll steal another witch, Mercy. And this time, it'll be an actual witch, and he's going to *kill* her to stuff her spirit into Morgan's dead body. If he doesn't have Morgan's body, then he has no one to do this ritual on," she said tearfully.

"Jax, do you know, did Evan kill Morgan Hartford?" I asked, making sure that Morgan was still out of the room.

"No, I'm pretty sure Evan and Freddy just stole the body. They aren't the murderers," Jax revealed.

With great fanfare, Sweets threw her arms up in the air. "Done!" she hollered and with her arm extended out in front of her she dropped the scissors on the floor as if she were the first to finish her math test.

Jax pulled her feet out of the cut ankle cuffs. "Thanks, Sweets! Alba, are you almost done with my wrist?"

Just then, Morgan appeared through the wall and back into the dungeon like room. "He's coming, Evan is coming!" Her voice was shaky, and I could tell that she was scared, despite the fact that she was already dead and a ghost.

"Morgan said he's here," I announced nervously. "Holly, get the light! Sweets, quick, get behind the door with me."

"Hurry Alba," Jax bawled, scared out of her mind.

"There, I've just about got it. Got it!"

Jax pulled her other wrist out of the cuff and Alba pulled her tiny frame quickly off of the table. The two of them joined me, Sweets, and Holly behind the door. Alba sucked in a deep breath and blew hard, snapping her fingers once again. The candles all flickered momentarily and then the room went dark.

We heard a rattle at the doorway, and then it slowly creaked open.

"I think I figured out what I did wrong, my little witch pop," said the deep male voice as he surged forward into the dark room, leaving the dungeon door open, letting in only a tiny sliver of light in the opposite direction of where we were hiding. When Jax didn't make a noise, he spoke into the darkness again. "Are you sleeping my little pumpkin?"

My little pumpkin? The words hung in the air, vowing to make me vomit on his shoes. The Witch Squad was finally reunited, huddled behind a door, under extremely unfortunate circumstances. We held our collective breath, scared to breathe, scared that he would hear us.

"You're so quiet tonight, my little Jaxie poo, what's the matter sugar plum? Cat got your tongue?" he said. He followed up his nauseating colloquialisms with a chuckle. We could hear him making his way towards the pull chain over the desk. We tried to smash ourselves against the wall as best as we could so that he wouldn't accidentally trip over one of our feet or brush up against anyone's arm or leg.

Our hearts were in our throats, and I wished that we had learned an invisibility spell over the past week. We could hear Evan bumbling around in the dark. Then the sound of the chain being discovered and then click – there we were, surrounded by light.

It took Evan only a second to notice that Jax wasn't on the table and by the time he had turned to look around the room, we were already making our way towards the other side of the door. In a flash, he drew his wand from the waistband of his cloak and with a tiny crackle, the door slammed shut.

"Well, helloooo," he purred. "What a nice surprise! Jaxie darling, you didn't tell me we were having guests. I would have made sure to have accommodations for everyone!"

Jax's bottom lip began to quiver. I squeezed her arm protectively.

"It's so nice of you ladies to join us. I was just going to put on a show! And your friend Jax was about to be the main event. Perhaps Jax told you, we had a few glitches earlier in the day, but I've just been to the wizard's library and I think I've figured out what I've been doing wrong."

"Let us out of here, Evan," I commanded, finally having had enough, I stepped forward with my chest puffed out as far as I could muster.

He began to laugh, a psychotic where's-my-straight-jacket, kind of laugh. "Oh, I'll let you out of here. Once I've stuffed all of your spirits inside of this body over here. You see, the Autumnal Equinox is nearing. And I have something especially wicked planned. I'm going to prove to everyone once and for all, who is *the most* talented wizard at this school," he droned.

We tried to keep our eyes glued to him, despite the fact that Alba was using her powers of telekinesis to raise the desk behind him high over his head. Slowly, it approached him.

"I'm going to get my name engraved on a stone in the lobby as student of the year, and I'll go on to do great things. All by making this single spell work. You see, I'm an innovative wizard, a visionary really…"

I shot him a broad sarcastic smile. "If you're such a visionary Evan, I guess you should have seen this one coming."

With that Alba dropped her fingers swiftly,

plummeting the heavy steel desk down on him hard. We watched as he crumpled to the floor in a heap under the desk.

"Hurry girls! Sweets, Holly, take Jax and get out of here!" I commanded. "Alba and I are going to work on getting Morgan's body out of here."

Sweets looked back nervously as Holly and Jax ran out the door. "Should I send help back, Mercy?"

"I think we've got it Sweets. I forgot we had a professional mover on staff," I said with a little wink at Alba.

"Ok, be careful!" Sweets hollered before escaping behind Holly and Jax.

"Let's get her uncovered," Alba said quickly.

I nodded, holding my breath, preparing myself for the gruesome sight of Morgan's corpse. I could see by the scrunched up look on Alba's face she was bracing herself for the sight as well. Standing on either side of the stainless steel table, we each took a side of the tarp and pulled it back, exposing the lifeless body.

"Oh, gosh. I just hate looking at myself like that," I heard Morgan say from behind me. I turned around to see the poor girl looking like she was crying, though as a ghost, no tears were able to fall.

"I'm sorry, Morgan, in all the chaos I forgot for a moment that you were still here. You should go. You don't need to see this. Please, go, follow my friends to safety. We will meet up later; we don't have much time. Evan could wake up. We need to get your body to safety, so your parents can have the closure to bury you properly.

"Ok," she said in a small voice as a little sob escaped her lips and with that she disappeared through the door.

"You're going to be able to float her out of here, right?" I asked Alba nervously.

Alba nodded seriously. "Yeah, I think I can, the problem is going to be getting her out of here unseen. And what do we do about Evan? We can't just let him get away with this."

"Let's get the body out of here, and then we'll see what we can do about him," I said, throwing Evan a nasty look. The sight of him made me sick.

"Ok," Alba agreed. She stood back and pointed her fingers towards the corpse, levitating her immediately. "It'll be interesting getting her up that circular stairway."

"I'll guide her, let's go," I said and started towards the open door.

All of a sudden, the door slammed shut in front of me. "Not so fast," we heard from behind us. Evan had crawled out from under the desk and was hunched over, leaning on the stone altar. His face was battered and bloodied, and his shirt was stained red. "What's your hurry?"

"We're getting a little tired of seeing your face," Alba said, her voice thick with annoyance. She rolled her eyes then moved her fingers downward, setting Morgan's body back where it had been.

"Oh, I'm so sorry to hear that," Evan scoffed, walking towards us.

I backed up, towards the door.

"Don't be sorry," Alba said, challenging him. She made a quick motion with her fingers and brought the heavy chandelier swinging towards him.

Evan lifted his arm, quickly deflecting the hit. "Oh, I'm on to you now, sister," he said with an evil smile.

Alba looked at me. I could see fear taking shape in her brown eyes. I scooted over closer to her, huddling by her side as Evan came closer. His wand pointed at us.

As he lifted the wand to cast a spell on us, we heard a crackling noise at the door. Our three sets of eyes all turned to the door and found that it was turning to ice! A foot from the other side suddenly came plunging through it, shattering the door into tiny shards of glass like ice, crumbling the door to the ground. The Ice Princess jumped across the threshold with the Fire Queen hot on her tail.

"Sup Evan," Libby said with a tough smile on her face and her flattened palms at the ready.

Evan grinned evilly at the dynamic duo. "Libs! So nice of you to join us! Cin, my favorite hottie, a pleasure as always."

"You guys know this clown?" Alba asked the twins.

"Yeah, we've had a few run in's. Let's just say he doesn't take rejection well," Libby said. "He just doesn't know when enough is enough."

Evan threw his head back and laughed. "Oh, puh-lease. You still think this is about *you*? I was never interested in you anyway. I just wanted to get you in bed."

"Exactly why we had to incinerate your bed." Without taking her eyes off of Evan, Cinder finished,

"Now, you girls look like you could use a little help."

"Definitely. How'd you know that we were down here?" I asked.

"The other half of the Witch Squad saw us as they were running inside. They told us you might need a little assistance," Libby revealed.

"Why don't the two of you get out of here," said Cinder. "We'll handle our old pal, Evan."

"Deal," I said.

Alba wasted no time in twitching her fingers, levitating Morgan's body off the table.

"Hold up. You're not going anywhere!" Evan hollered and shot a stream of energy directly at Alba, but the twins' reflexes were faster.

Cinder deflected Evan's stream of energy by shooting a stream of fire from her finger. Libby covered Evan from head to toe in ice, freezing him solid.

"It's as easy as giving a kid a piece of candy on Halloween," Cinder said with a laugh.

"We'll watch him," Libby said. "You guys go."

"Thanks, girls, we appreciate it!" I told them. "Let's go, Alba. We need to get this body out of here!"

Together, Alba and I worked the body up the spiral staircase. "What are we going to do with her?" Alba asked.

I couldn't think. My nerves were completely shot. "I have no idea. We can't very well take her to the police station. Stone would kill us!"

"Yeah, and what are we supposed to do about Evan? We can't just let him get away with kidnapping Jax," Alba added.

Then it hit me, like a lightning bolt. "I've got it. I know the perfect place to put her body!" I said excitedly.

CHAPTER NINETEEN

I pulled out my cell phone and quickly dialed the Paranormal Institute's operator.

"Paranormal Institute for Witchcraft and Wizardry, how may I direct your call?" the nasally voice on the other end said.

"Warner Hall please," I said.

"Hold please."

"What are you doing?" Alba hissed at me at the top of the basement stairs.

"Shh," I whispered back, with a hand over the mouthpiece of my phone.

"Information, may I help you?"

"Yes, hello. I'd like to send my son a care package. He lives in Warner Hall. Could you please give me his room number?"

"Yes, ma'am. What's your son's name?" she asked

politely. I could hear her clicking the buttons on a computer.

"Evan. Evan Lancaster," I said, excitedly.

"Lancaster, yes, here he is. Room 323. Can I help you with anything else?" she asked.

"No, thank you, that's all I needed." I smiled through the phone at her.

"You're welcome, have a nice day."

I hung up the phone while Alba smiled broadly at me. "Room 323, piece of cake."

"I've got to give you credit, Red, that was a brilliant idea."

I grinned from ear to ear. "Thanks, I know. Come on, let's go. We can't have someone see us."

Getting Morgan's lifeless body up the stairs via levitation was more difficult than one might think. She didn't bend around the corners very easily.

"I hope you're a better furniture mover than you are a body mover," I said sarcastically to Alba after she'd knocked Morgan's head on the stone wall at least a half a dozen times. She was good at lifting, but her accuracy left a lot to be desired.

Within fifteen minutes, we had stowed away Morgan's body in Evan's dorm room, without having been seen. Once we got safe and sound back to Winston Hall, I made one more phone call – an anonymous call to the Aspen Falls Police Department.

"Yes, hello. I'd like to report that a body was just discovered at the Warner Hall dormitory. Room 323. Please hurry."

I hung up the phone and turned to Alba quickly. "There, hopefully, the girls will keep Evan on ice until Morgan's body is recovered!"

"And hopefully no one will be the wiser that it was us calling it in."

"Exactly! Now, we've got to get upstairs. I'm dying to know if Jax is going to be alright," I said.

"Let's go," said Alba.

Jax was sitting on the edge of my bed weeping when we came in. Sneaks was sitting next to her, patting her back gently. I rushed to her side and knelt down next to the bed. "Jax, are you alright? Should we take you to the infirmary?" I asked her immediately.

She sniffed her nose and wiped at her eyes. "No, I'm not hurt. It was just so, scary!" she cried.

"Aww, poor Jaxie," Sweets cooed while hugging her tightly.

Sneaks wrapped herself around Jax's leg and purred softly. When she saw me, my mother sighed. "There you are! I've been worried sick!"

I knelt in front of Jax and took her hands into mine, ignoring my mother. She winced as I turned her wrists over to get a good look at them. They were bruised and swollen and cut in several places from her trying to pull herself loose all day. "You're bleeding," I said. "Does anyone have a first aid kit?"

"I've got some stuff in our room, I'll be right back," said Holly as she ran out quickly.

"I'm just so confused about what's going on," I admitted. "If Evan didn't kill Morgan, then do we know who did?" I asked Jax.

"I have no idea who killed Morgan," Jax said sadly. "I wish I knew, but I don't."

I stood up and turned around to face Morgan, who was standing quietly in the corner of my room. "We haven't had a chance to meet formally. I'm Mercy," I told her.

"Hi Mercy," she said shyly.

"I saw you on the side of the road the day that you were killed," I said.

"I saw you there too, and the rest of these girls," she admitted.

"This is Alba and Sweets. And obviously you know this is Jax," I said as Holly entered the room with her first aid kid. "And this is Holly."

Holly looked around curiously. "Who are you talking to?"

"Morgan. She's here," I said.

"Oh, tell her I said hi," she said with a little wave. "And tell her I'm sorry she died."

"She can hear you," I pointed out. "You just can't hear her."

"Oh. Hi Morgan, I'm sorry you died," Holly said loudly into the room.

"She's a ghost, Holly. She's not deaf," I said with a chuckle.

"Sorry," Holly said as she squatted down to help Jax clean up her wrists.

"Morgan, do you know who did this to you?" I asked her cautiously. I wasn't sure what she knew yet.

Sometimes ghosts remembered every detail and sometimes they didn't. Often it just took time, and they remembered everything.

Morgan shook her head and looked at her hands nervously. "No. I don't know. I've tried to remember that day, but I can't remember anything. It's like it's being blocked from my memory or something."

Jax finally spoke up. "I feel like this has something to do with the Autumnal Equinox celebration. I feel like she was supposed to be a sacrifice."

"That thought had crossed my mind," I admitted.

"It did? Why?" Morgan asked, looking up in surprise.

"We found your ring," I told her.

She looked down at her hands and saw that it was missing. "My ring? How did you know I had a ring?"

"We went back to look for you. And we found your ring on the side of the road. It's a purity ring, right?"

She nodded.

"That means – "

"Yes. It means I'm a virgin," she admitted shyly.

I smiled at her as kindly as I could. "There are a lot of rituals in the spiritual world that require the sacrifice of a virgin."

"Oh," she whispered. "So it was a witch that killed me?"

"Not necessarily. We think it was a man. It might have been a wizard that killed you."

"You think it was Evan?" she asked fearfully.

"Jax doesn't think so. There are other wizards living in Aspen Falls. It could have been someone else."

She nodded, but I could tell that she was biting her bottom lip.

"Are you alright?" I asked her.

She shook her head, trying to hold back the tears that would never fall again. "No. Honestly, I'm not alright. It stinks. I saved myself for marriage, and it got me killed. How is that right?"

I wished that I could reach out and touch her, comfort her, but I knew I couldn't. Her body wasn't concrete. It was only her spirit that was present. "It's not right, Morgan. I'm so sorry."

"If she was killed because she was a virgin that means whoever killed her had to have known her. How else would they know that she was a virgin?" Alba cleverly pointed out.

"Who knew you were a virgin, Morgan?" I asked her.

"Most of my girlfriends knew," she said.

I swished my lips to the side. "Eh, we're pretty sure it was a man."

"Sam knew, but I don't think that he would ever hurt me. He loved me. I'm sure this is really hard on him," she said, choking up.

"He's pretty devastated. So are your parents," I told her. "We met them."

"You met my mom and dad? When? How are they? I miss them so much!" Morgan's face crumpled at the mere mention of her family.

"After we saw you at the crime scene, we went to the school. They were pretty distraught," I said. "Who else knew you were a virgin?"

"My parents knew and my youth group knew. All of us girls wore the same purity rings," she said.

"You mean you all wore a purity ring?" I asked, seeking clarification. "But not *the same* purity ring, right?"

"No, we all had the *exact same* ring. It was a gift from our youth group counselor."

"What's she saying?" Alba asked me curiously.

"She said that all of the kids in her youth group wore the exact same ring. She said it was a gift from their youth group counselor."

"Who was their youth group counselor?" Alba asked.

I turned around and looked at Morgan curiously.

"Mr. Bushwhack," she said.

"Oliver Bushwhack?" I asked, astounded.

"Yeah, Oliver," she said, surprised. "You know him?"

"We met him the day you were killed. He was in the office comforting your parents," I told her, then I spun around to tell the rest of the girls what Morgan had said. "Guys, Oliver Bushwhack was her youth group counselor."

"So?" Holly asked.

"We met him. He was in the office consoling Morgan's mother," I reminded them.

"And? Why do you seem so surprised that he was the youth group counselor?" Holly asked. "He was introduced as the Guidance Counselor."

"I'm not surprised that he is the youth group counselor, but isn't it more than a little odd that a male youth group counselor gave a bunch of girls a purity ring?" I asked. Something just wasn't making any sense.

"It just seems kind of creepy to me."

Suddenly a light seemed to click on over Alba's head. "Oh, my gosh! I just thought of something!"

"What is it?" Sweets asked anxiously.

"Where is it?" Alba asked looking around the room like a mad woman.

"What are you looking for?" I asked her, confused.

"Here it is!" she announced, holding up the yearbook we found in the attic earlier in the day.

"What's that?" Jax asked.

"It's an old yearbook. Stone locked us in the tower last night. This morning we found a secret passageway and crawled up to the attic. Mercy and I found this up there," said Alba.

"Well, what's that got to do with any of this?" Jax asked confused.

Alba flipped through the pages quickly. "We saw a picture…here!" she said, slamming her pointer finger down just above the picture. "Look!"

There it was in black and white: *BethAnn and Oliver enjoy the Autumnal Equinox celebration in the town square.* "That's *got* to be the same Oliver," she said triumphantly.

Jax's eyes widened when she saw the black and white picture in front of her. "And that's The Black Witch!" she said.

"What?!" I demanded, falling to my knees to look at the picture too.

"Yeah, BethAnn. That's the Black Witch's name," Jax said as plain as day.

"How do you know that?" Holly asked uncertainly.

"I saw her picture hanging somewhere. She used to go to this school," said Jax, closing the book and gesturing towards the cover. "Obviously. They are in a Paranormal Institute yearbook."

"What year is the yearbook?"I asked.

"1936," said Jax, reading from the cover.

"How old do you think he was in that picture?" I asked the girls.

Jax shrugged. "I don't know. I would guess he was 20."

"Ok, for easy math's sake, let's say Oliver was 20 in 1936, that means he was born in 1916, and so he'd have to be around a hundred year's old right now, right?" I asked.

The girls nodded at my rationalization.

"He didn't look like he was over one hundred when we met him," Holly said.

"Exactly. Are we sure that this is a picture of him?" I asked and flipped open the book to scrutinize the picture once again.

"It looks like Mr. Bushwhack," Morgan admitted, looking over our shoulder at the black and white photo.

"Morgan says it looks like him," I said to the girls.

"So Oliver Bushwhack and the Black Witch dated?" Sweets asked, confused. "That's so bizarre. I wonder what that means."

"Well, I hate to state the obvious, but I think it means that Oliver Bushwhack is a paranormal," I pointed out.

Jax and Holly nodded.

"He's got to be," said Alba.

Morgan shook her head. "Wow, I just can't believe it! All that time Mr. Bushwhack was a paranormal, and we never knew!"

"So he makes sure that the girls in the youth group all take a purity vow," I started to work it all out aloud.

"They remain virgins until he can kill one of them for a sacrifice on the Autumnal Equinox," Alba says, taking over my thought process.

"It makes sense," Jax said.

Morgan's head shook back and forth as if she couldn't believe what we were proposing.

"Well, then why would he kill Morgan on the side of the road?" Sweets finally asked.

I glanced at Morgan again. She was in a trance, watching something replay in her memory.

"Are we triggering a flashback, Morgan?" I asked nervously.

"I can see him," she said fearfully. Her hand once again fingered the small cross at her neckline.

"Who can you see?" I asked her.

The girls turned to look at me.

"I think she's having a breakthrough," I whispered.

"Oliver. On the side of the road. He offered to give me a ride home," she said, fear biting through her voice.

"But I said, 'No, thank you. I'm almost home.'"

"And then what?" I prodded.

"And then he said that he insisted. I said, I was almost home, and I'd just drive my dad's truck back to school, but then he pulled the car over to the side of the road," she choked back her frightened sobs while she relived the terrifying experience in her mind.

"He got out of the car and came towards me. I just kind of laughed at him; I thought he was trying to be funny. Like pretending he was going to grab me, but then he actually grabbed me. And I screamed! I tried to get free. We wrestled around, but he had a knife in his pocket," she cried. "And he held it to my throat and told me to get in the car. I started to, but then I decided he wouldn't stab me. I knew him. He was my teacher. He would never hurt me, so I tried to get loose. I pulled away from him."

"It's okay, Morgan," I said quietly, feeling a huge lump in the back of my throat as I tried to swallow. "You don't have to say it."

She shook her head violently as the story continued to play out in her mind. It was as if she were seeing the whole thing for the first time. "I pulled away from him, and he came after me again and we fought and then I felt the knife, and I saw blood …and then…and then…everything went black," she finished and began to sob.

"Oh, Morgan. What a tragic story, I'm so sorry for what you went through," I consoled her. I only wished that I could hug her and help her to feel better. Then and there I vowed to learn to be able to physically touch a spirit.

"What did she say?" Alba asked quietly.

"It was Oliver." I hung my head sadly. "She remembered everything. He was trying to abduct her, but she tried to get away, and they wrestled, and he had a knife, and well, you know how it ended."

The girls all bowed their heads sadly. We were all quiet for several long moments, each of us lost in our own thoughts.

"What do we do now?" Holly finally asked.

Alba shook her head. "I really don't know. Do we go to Stone?"

"We can't go to Stone. She just threatened to kick us out of The Institute if we keep getting involved in Morgan's murder. I can't afford to get kicked out of college!" I insisted. As much as I'd love to never have to go to school another day in my life, I knew that I couldn't return to Dubbsburg until I could prove I'd gotten my gift under control. And suddenly I wanted to do just that, more than anything else. I wanted to learn to use my gift for a greater purpose.

"You don't think she'd want to know that we solved the murder?" Alba asked wearily.

Morgan moved closer to me. "Mercy, there were at least six other girls in my youth group that Mr. Bushwhack gave purity rings to. Do you think it's possible that he'll go after one of them before the celebration tonight?"

"I think it's entirely possible," I said to her and then turned to the girls. "Morgan said there are six other girls in her youth group that were given purity rings by Oliver. What if he's going to go after one of them before the Equinox celebration tonight?"

"They are all in grave danger!" Jax said, fear evident in her voice.

Finally, Sneaks, who had decided to hang back and pretend like she was sleeping walked towards me. "I told you Mercy. I knew it. Those girls are in danger, but so are you and these girls."

"Mom, hush, we're trying to figure this out."

"Mom?" Jax asked confused. "Mercy did you just call the cat, Mom?"

"She can talk to the cat now," Sweets shared excitedly.

"What?" Holly's eyes shot open wide as she spun around. "When did you learn to do that?"

"While you were out after your vision," I explained.

"So, you renamed her Mom?" Jax asked, shaking her head.

"No," I said with a nervous laugh. "The cat is my mom. My mom is the cat. She did a spell. She's spying on me."

"I am not spying on you, Mercy! Stop saying that!"

"You are too, Mom," I said rolling my eyes. "She says she's not spying, but I know she is."

"That's so cool," Holly said, looking at Sneaks.

"Sorry, can we get back to Oliver?" I asked impatiently.

"I know Stone doesn't want us to, but we've got to alert the Aspen Falls PD," said Alba.

Holly nodded in agreement. "We can't just sit around and do nothing and let that monster claim another innocent victim!"

"Stone would kill us!" I disagreed.

"We could call in another anonymous tip," Alba

suggested.

"Would they believe us?" Holly asked.

"I think we've got to try, what do we have to lose?" Alba concluded.

CHAPTER TWENTY

After placing a second anonymous call into the Aspen Falls PD and warning them that Oliver Bushwhack was Morgan Hartford's killer and encouraging them to make sure all girls in his youth group were safe and accounted for, we took a break to get ready for the Autumnal Equinox town's celebration.

We had no choice but to go to the town event, if for no other reason than to make sure the citizens of Aspen Falls were protected. Hopefully, by the time it started, Oliver Bushwhack would be safely stowed away in police custody.

The girls had all gone back to their rooms to take a little nap and recover from the whole Evan situation, and Morgan had decided to take a bit of time to herself to wander the campus and get her emotions under control.

I'd asked Mom to give me a little bit of space and come back later, and thankfully she'd obliged. The Witch Squad planned to meet back up for supper in the courtyard together before we headed over to the street dance. Jax and I finally had a little breather and time to talk privately. It saddened me that my usual, bubbly little elf was extremely unbubbly and uncharacteristically quiet.

"Jax, can we talk?" I asked her quietly, casting my green eyes guiltily towards the floor.

She shrugged lightly as she sat quietly at her desk, scrolling through pictures on the Witchgram App on her phone. I pulled my chair up close to hers and watched her for a moment, trying desperately to come up with any words that would make it right between the two of us again.

"Jax, I don't know where to start. I don't know how to make this right," I finally began uncomfortably. "What I said the other day…how I treated you. I was terrible."

"Mercy, you don't have to…" she interrupted calmly.

"But I do, Jax! When I got here, you were the sweetest, most sincerely *nice* person to me. You were eager and excited and accepting, and I just stomped all over that. I was the opposite. I treated you terribly, and I regret it so badly."

"Thanks, Mercy, I appreciate the apology."

"It's not just that, Jax. I feel *horrible* about the things I said to you when you told us you weren't a witch. Just because I don't want to be one, doesn't mean that others don't want to either. And your family is all witches. Of course, you have every right to have the need to be accepted by your own family, and I mocked that. And I hurt you. I'm so sorry," I said, tears streamed down my face by now.

Jax still hadn't turned around to face me. Instead, a fat tear began to fall down her cheeks as well. She wiped them away and then finally turned to look me in the eye. "Mercy, what I don't understand is, why wouldn't you want the amazing gift you've been given? Look at how you've been able to help Morgan, and we're going to get a *murderer* off the streets because of *you!* Don't you see how amazing that is? And how *brave* you are?"

I looked down at my lap. No one had ever called me brave before or told me that my gift was *amazing*. I didn't know what to say. I splayed my hands out in front of me and shrugged. "I'm not brave," I finally managed.

Jax turned her chair around, so our bodies were squared up. "But you are brave. You led the girls down to a *dungeon* to save me, Mercy. That is so incredibly brave. I don't think I would have been brave enough to do that on my own. I would have followed you, but I wouldn't have led the group. You're a natural born leader."

"Jax, you're too nice. I'm not a good person," I croaked out, swallowing back the lump in my throat, trying not to bawl like a four-year-old.

"Mercy Habernackle! Don't say that! You are a very good person," Jax argued. "I don't care what happened back home. You were just misunderstood. Different doesn't mean bad. It just means misunderstood. You're a good person here," she said. "And here." She reached out and touched her finger to my heart, making it even more difficult to keep my tears reserved.

"You're too nice to me, Jax. I really don't deserve it. I almost got you killed," I said, sniffling.

"*You* didn't almost get me killed. Freddy almost got me killed, and *Evan* almost got me killed," she insisted. "Speaking of Freddy, we need to do some serious spells on that jerk. Know any good witches who do voodoo?" she said laughing while brushing at her tear stained face.

"I know a witch who knows a witch," I told her with a broad smile.

"Ok, now no more talk about this being your fault, understand?" she asked me seriously.

I nodded. "Yeah, alright. But no more talk about me being a good person," I added.

She giggled. "Just as long as you remember that you are, I'll try to quit reminding you. But no more talk about not wanting to be a witch. While you're here, I want you to think of those that don't have your gifts," she said pointing to herself. "And I want you to appreciate your life and your gifts and your mother and especially *your friends*. Because we're here for you."

"Ok. Now, we should get ready, because after the day that I've had, I'm *starving*."

"*You're* starving? I haven't eaten in *forever*," said Jax, rumbling around through her mini fridge. "I had a few bottles of orange juice in here, but I don't see them. Did you happen to take them?"

I smiled. "We'll blame those on Holly," I said with a laugh. "Now, let's get going!"

***

By the way that Holly's 'girls' were heaved up in her shirt like masts on a sailboat, I could only assume that she was hoping to bump into Alex, the guy from the morgue, at the Autumnal Equinox celebration in the town square. "I take it you're not broken-hearted over Evan?" I asked her as Jax and I joined the girls at their table in the courtyard that evening.

The sun was low on the horizon, and there was a faint cool breeze rustling a pile of dead leaves that had collected next to the low stone wall. I had opted for the warm and cozy look this evening, wearing a long rust colored duster sweater over my usual black t-shirt and a pair of skinny jeans with my black Converse sneakers.

Holly fluttered her fake eyelashes and gave me a whimsical smile. "Oh, gosh, who's Evan?" she said with a laugh. "I'm looking forward to having a little fun after all of this serious stuff we've had to deal with."

"Me too," said Jax. "The last 24 hours has been brutal. I want to enjoy the celebration tonight! And I can't wait to eat! I'm starving!" She dove into her plate, eating more than I'd ever seen Jax eat in the past.

"Where's Alba?" I asked, looking around.

"She's coming. She went to make sure that Libby and Cinder are alright and that Evan got what was coming to him," Holly said with a harrumph.

"Good. Sweets, you're being awfully quiet." Looking down the table at Sweets, I noticed she was sitting with her back unusually straight and staring off into the distance as if she were daydreaming.

Upon hearing my voice, she shook her head as if clearing the cobwebs out of her mind and then she trained her deep eyes on mine. "I think I just had a premonition."

I looked around to the other girls' faces. "I didn't know you had premonitions, Sweets."

"I don't have premonitions. I've never had one before. Maybe I was just daydreaming," she said, unconvinced about her own vision. She shook her head again and then speared another bite of food.

"It could have been a premonition, Sweets. What did you see?" I asked her with interest.

"I saw a storm cloud above Aspen Falls and a raging fire. I saw Oliver's evil face laughing. The feeling that I got was that no one is safe," she said tentatively.

I shot Jax a furtive glance. If Sweet's vision was real and we were in for a firestorm, I wasn't entirely sure that Jax should go to the Equinox celebration with us after all. After everything she'd just gone through, perhaps she wasn't ready to handle it if something happened.

"Jax – " I began before she cut me off.

"I'm going, Mercy. There's no way I'm not going. We need to make sure that those girls are all safe."

"What girls?" Alba asked, as she sat down her try and slid in next to Jax.

"The youth group girls. Sweets had a vision about Oliver. She doesn't think anyone is safe," said Jax.

"Since when do you have visions, Sweets?" Alba

asked, confused.

Sweets threw up her hands. "I don't know? I just had one. Maybe it's nothing. Don't mind me. I'll just be over here eating this pumpkin spice bar with cream cheese frosting…mmm, these are good. Has anyone tried these yet?"

I had to laugh. Leave it to Sweets to divert serious talk with frivolous food talk. "Sweets, stop. Don't dismiss your vision. Just because you haven't had one before doesn't mean it's not real. We are all learning about our powers and abilities. That's the point of college, right? To grow as witches?"

She shrugged and licked off the white frosting. "Mm-hmm, I suppose."

"Alright, we need to go tonight prepared and alert," I asserted. I turned to Alba. "Well, what's the status on the twins and Evan?"

Alba swallowed her bite of food and then beamed at us. "They recovered Morgan's body. Evan was found, chilling on ice in the basement of Warner Hall. Cinder and Libby were nowhere near him when he was found, but I did talk to them, and they are both just fine. They said they heard that Evan was being arrested and he's already been kicked out of school."

"Witch bump," I said and held my fist out to each girl to bump. "That's awesome!"

"Yay!" Jax cheered. "Oh! I feel *so* much better! Now all we have to do is deal with Freddy, and I'll feel amazing!"

"Oh, I talked to Libby and Cinder about Freddy.

They're going to take care of him, too. I don't think you'll have to worry about him *ever* again," Alba added with a wicked grin.

Jax leaned over and threw her arms around Alba excitedly. "Oh! How can I ever thank you! You girls are the best friends I've ever had. Just ever! I love you all so much," she gushed.

Despite the fact that I wasn't into gooey mushy love stuff, Jax's bubbly energy made me smile. I finally felt like the old Jax had returned. Alba patted Jax's arm, rolling her eyes lightly. It was obvious that she was uncomfortable with the very public display of affection from Jax, but just like we all felt, Jax was growing on us.

CHAPTER TWENTY-ONE

By 8:00 we were standing in the center of the Aspen Falls street dance. There was a live band on stage, playing a mix of rock and roll and country music. Under other circumstances, I could have listened to it all night long; it was totally my type of music. The air had gotten cooler as the sun finally dipped below the horizon. The downtown was lit by colorful hanging pumpkin lights and lanterns and the scent of street vendors selling a variety of delicious items like funnel cakes and walking tacos filled the air. The lights on the waterfall in the center of town had been turned on, illuminating the falling water into brilliant fall colors.

Walking between Jax and Alba, I pulled my sweater around me tighter to keep out the cool night air. It seemed it was going to be cooler than I had originally intended as a shiver crawled down either side of my legs, pebbling my skin. Our string of pretty young women caught the attention of several male admirers as we moved through the crowds towards the stage area. Holly nodded at each admirer in turn and shot the cute ones interested winks, hoping that one would come ask her to dance.

Suddenly a pair of figures working a fundraiser next to the police station caught my eye. "Girls, I'll be back in a minute," I hollered to my friends and then motioned for Morgan to follow me.

"Where are we going?" Morgan asked, floating carefully through the crowd as if she were going to bump elbows with a mortal, accidentally.

"You'll see," I said with a light smile.

Once the crowd parted slightly and Morgan was able to see up ahead, she sucked in her breath. "Mom! Dad!" she said excitedly. "Oh, Mercy, that's my mom and dad!"

"I know," I said just loud enough to be heard over the music. "I saw them. I thought maybe you'd like to stay with them for awhile?"

Surprisingly, Morgan's ghostly face flushed at the sight of her family, and I knew she'd easily cry if she had any tears to cry. I thought it important that she have an opportunity to say goodbye to her parents before her time as a ghost expired. Which, in my experience, was when her duties on Earth were resolved. And I was very hopeful that by having Oliver Bushwhack in police custody and having recovered Morgan's body, we'd have given Morgan's spirit an opportunity to be at peace, finally. I still wasn't sure why she hadn't disappeared already.

"Thanks, Mercy," she said. "You're amazing. I can't thank you enough for what you've done for me."

It was a rare thing that anyone thanked me for anything. Anywhere else, my gifts were looked at as a curse. I was finally starting to appreciate Aspen Falls for the accepting place that it was.

"They won't be able to see you, you know," I warned her as she approached them.

She turned around and gave me a broad smile. "I know. But I'm able to see them. That's enough for me."

I waved goodbye to her and wandered back through the crowd to find the girls. As I did, one man, in particular, caught my eye.

"Detective Whitman!" I called loudly over the booming of the speakers not far away.

"Mercy," he said with a little nod and an ever so slight grin. "Enjoying a night out?"

I tilted my head to the side with a mischievous little smile. "The girls and I will enjoy it better when we know that you got our gift," I hollered over the music.

"Your gift?" The confusion in his face didn't sit right with me, and I immediately felt my stomach drop.

"The anonymous tip about Morgan's killer? You got it right?"

"That was you that called in the anonymous tip?" he asked with shock.

I nodded. "Yeah, the girls and I figured out the murderer. And we recovered Morgan's body!" I said triumphantly.

"Mercy, why wouldn't you come to me yourself? Why call it in as an anonymous tip?" His body language changed so dramatically that I knew something was up. If everything was wrapped up and in the bag, why would he be so suddenly jumpy?

"I don't know. Maybe because you tell Stone every time we so much as breathe? And maybe because Stone has promised to expel us from The Institute if we continued to investigate Morgan's death or spoke to you regarding the case in any way. And really, you're not very receptive to leads anyway, so why would we tell you it was us that solved the case?" *What other reason do we need?* I wondered. "Now, who cares about all of that? We served Oliver Bushwhack up to you on a platter. How about a thank you?"

Detective Whitman's face paled. I looked at him curiously.

"You've put all of the students in his youth group under surveillance for the evening right?" I asked nervously.

"I didn't know that tip came from you," he stuttered.

"You're freaking me out here, Detective! Tell me you've got Oliver Bushwhack under arrest! Tell me those girls are all safe and accounted for!" I hollered, my face filling with blood.

"We had no evidence to arrest him," he finally stammered out. "And Morgan Hartford's body was discovered in Evan Lancaster's dorm room."

"Evan Lancaster didn't kill Morgan Hartford!"

"So he said. We are still investigating," said Detective

Whitman.

"Investigating what? There's nothing to investigate! We solved the case for you. We called in the killer!"

"I was sure Evan was lying," he admitted.

"But you've got the girls under surveillance?" I asked.

"There's no proof that he's going to harm those girls!"

I face palmed myself and then looked up at Detective Whitman. I decided to take a chance, taking into account everything that Jax had taught me and everything this town was teaching me. I decided to use my gift. If it didn't work and a mortal tried to lock me away in a mental institution somewhere again, well, then I'd never speak of my gifts again, and I guess I'd learn to love white coats. But in that moment, I didn't hesitate to put the youth group girls' lives above mine. "Detective Whitman. I'm going to share something with you. Something that few people know and few people approve of. And I want you to trust me. Because I'm going to tell you the God's honest truth. Also, I'm going to need to trust you. Trust isn't something that I've been able to give many people in my life. Can I trust you?"

His eyes squinted as he peered at me closely. Perhaps he was considering whether or not I was crazy, or whether or not he should tell Stone that I was having this conversation with him, maybe he was even regretting coming to the celebration, but strangely enough, he nodded at me. "Yeah, yeah. I'll trust you Mercy. And you can trust me. Ok?"

I took a deep breath and shook the nerves out of my

wound-up body. "Detective Whitman. I have a gift. I can see ghosts. I've been able to see ghosts since I was a toddler, maybe younger. And Morgan Hartford's ghost is here tonight. She's standing right over there," I said and pointed towards her parents at the school fundraiser next to the police department. "She's seeing her parents for the first time since she was killed. And she clearly remembers who killed her. She *told me* it was Oliver, Detective."

I saw him flinch momentarily.

"In addition, my friends and I found an old Institute yearbook from 1936. Oliver Bushwhack was in that yearbook. He was in his early 20's. That was eighty years ago. Eighty years ago, he was 20, which would mean that right now, he is over one hundred years old. Now, I don't know about you, but when I met Mr. Bushwhack the day of the murder, he didn't look a day older than fifty. How does a 100-year-old man, look younger than 50? Either he's got some *amazing* face cream, or we can safely assume that Oliver Bushwhack is of the paranormal persuasion. But wait, there's more!" I said, holding up my pointer finger, "Morgan *told* us that he gave her that purity ring and he gave all the other girls in his youth group a purity ring too. Now, why would he do that, Detective?"

Detective Whitman looked down at the ground. Suddenly he was interested in the paved road he was standing on.

"I'll tell you why. Because he was preserving virgins. He wasn't supposed to kill Morgan Hartford on the side of the road that day. He was only supposed to abduct her and keep her until tonight, the Autumnal Equinox when he could sacrifice a virgin for whatever spell he's trying to perform. But guess what? He didn't *get* to keep Morgan Hartford. So I *promise you*, Detective. He will *get* another girl."

Finally, the detective pulled himself up straight and met my eyes head on. "I'm sorry I gave you so many reasons not to trust me, Mercy. But I trust you, and I'll take care of this. We will keep those girls safe," he promised.

"Good, there's no time to lose. It's going to happen tonight."

"Don't worry, I'll take care of it," he assured and quickly got out his cell phone, and rushed off towards the police department. "Mercy, thank you!"

I was stunned. He believed me. And I wasn't being led away in handcuffs – *that* was a welcome change from my life back home. Now, on to find the rest of the Witch Squad and fill them in on what was happening. I turned around and suddenly a big gust of wind swept through the streets. "Brr," I chattered loudy. "The weather's really changing quickly." I pulled my sweater around me even tighter and walked off in search of the girls.

I found Alba, standing alone in the crowd, with her arms crossed and an annoyed look cast upon her face. "What's wrong, Alba?" I asked.

She tipped her head in the direction of the stage. I turned and watched as Jax, Sweets, and Holly cut loose. "Why haven't you joined them?" I asked Alba with a little smile.

She only rolled her eyes at me. The wind whipped past us both again. "Boy, it's really getting chilly out," I said, looking up at the dark clouds rolling in. "Looks like a storm is coming."

"Took you long enough," Alba growled at me.

"I just got done talking to Detective Whitman. I wanted to make sure that the Aspen Falls PD had arrested Oliver. They haven't," I said angrily.

Alba's disinterested eyes suddenly lit up. "Oliver is still free? But they have those girls somewhere safe, right?"

I shook my head. "He didn't take the anonymous tip seriously. They thought Evan did it and was lying about murdering Morgan."

"So now what?" she asked.

"He believes us now. He just went back to the station. They are going to find Oliver."

"Good, time to put that creep away!" Alba looked up at the sky. "I think you're right, Red. I think there might be a storm rolling in. Maybe we should get the girls and head home before it catches us in the middle of it."

We could hear a rumbling off in the distance. The wind whipped around us again, throwing a torrent of dead leaves into the sky, they spun around our ankles as if they were caught in a twister.

"Yeah, the wind is really coming up!" I hollered. "Let's go."

Alba and I pulled the girls out of the mosh pit dance floor. "What?" Holly asked, slightly perturbed.

"It's going to storm; we need to get out of here!" I hollered.

"We just got here!" she whined.

Then a big fat raindrop splatted on her nose. She looked up to the sky, and before she could say *rain*, the sky cracked and popped over our head and burst loose into a torrential downpour.

People everywhere began screaming and running for shelter. The band frantically began trying to cover their equipment from the onslaught of rain and the people from the food trucks emerged to pull their awnings in and cover their open windows.

"Come on!" Alba hollered, through the thunder and lightning and crazy wind. "We've got to go!"

We had gotten to the event so late in the evening that our car was parked a million miles away on a side street, so by the time we got there, our clothes were completely soaking wet.

"That storm came out of nowhere!" Jax cried as she pulled the last car door shut, slamming us all inside.

The goosebumps that had plagued me earlier were back, and I shivered like I was coming down with pneumonia. "Sweets! P-p-put the h-h-heater on p-p-please! I'm f-f-freezing," I chattered.

"Heat, coming up!" she called as she maneuvered us off of the side street without hitting any of the hundreds of pedestrians that were racing to their cars.

"Something feels unnatural about this storm," Alba commented as she stared up at the dark storm clouds. "They are moving so quickly."

I looked up too. She was right. They were all moving swiftly towards what appeared to be the epicenter of the storm, which happened to be right above the Black Witch's private abode.

Holly noticed it immediately too. "The clouds all seem to be gathering over the Black Witch's house. Maybe she is the one responsible for this storm!"

"Could be," Alba agreed. "Let's check it out!"

Sweets watched the sky ahead as she drove. "I see black smoke up there, too. I definitely don't think this is nature's storm we're dealing with. It's got to be a paranormal storm. Someone is behind this."

"Are you going to be alright, Mercy?" Jax asked me, rubbing my arms and legs with her hands.

I nodded my head as best as I could, but my chills were only magnified the closer we got to the Black Witch. As we watched the rolling thunderheads gathering over her house, it became only too obvious that it wasn't pneumonia I was dealing with. Evil was near.

CHAPTER TWENTY-TWO

The rain stopped as we pulled into the Black Witch's long, dark, winding driveway. Though we could hear the storm rumbling back in town, it was eerily quiet the minute our tires pulled onto the gravel path to her house. The five of us shared several long moments of silence as Sweets stopped the car. Knowing very little about the Black Witch, I was sure we were all thinking the same thing, *Should we really be here right now?*

"I'm just gonna say it. I'm slightly freaked out right now," Sweets said nervously, turning to Alba in the front seat with fearful eyes.

"I think we're all a little freaked out right now," Holly assured her as she peered out her closed window towards the billowing smoke up ahead.

I reached out, putting a clammy hand on Sweets' shoulder. "Just drive, Sweets. We're all together. We'll be fine. Turn off your headlights."

She nodded vigorously as if trying to convince herself, and then let her foot off of the brake while flipping the lights off. We rolled ahead slowly, inches at a time. Alba slowly turned to eye Sweets. "Gas, Sweets!" Alba barked.

"Gas, yeah," she repeated nervously, and the car surged forward faster. The closer we got to the black billowing smoke, the harder Holly squeezed my hand in the back seat. I threw her a quick glance and noticed that her blue eyes were frantic.

"Holly, we're going to be ok," I assured her.

"I'm not getting a good feeling about this," she admitted.

"Oh really? You've got a bad feeling? What was it, Holly?" I asked her sarcastically. "Was it that freak storm we just went through? Perhaps it was the killer on the loose? Or maybe the fact that we're on the Black Witch's property? Or could you possibly be worried that Stone is going to kick us out of The Institute?"

Jax shot me the stink eye. "Mercy Habernackle! I thought you were going to start being nice!"

I threw my hands up. "Sorry, sorry. Sarcasm comes naturally to me. I'm working on it." I looked at Holly apologetically. "Sorry, Holly. You're right. None of us have a good feeling about this."

The car finally pulled up to a tall country cottage style castle, with twin towers that rose high into the sky and were covered with twisted layers of overgrown branches from a climbing plant of some sort. The windows were dark and I silently wondered if the Black Witch was even home.

"The smoke isn't even coming from above her house like we thought," Alba observed. "It's coming from behind her house. Can we drive back that way?"

"We can try," Sweets said and followed a narrow dirt path that seemed to wrap around her house and lead towards the field just beyond it.

As the house moved out of our line of sight, we were able to see an enormous bonfire roaring in the field behind the Black Witch's castle. A dark figure loomed in front of us facing the fire, fanning the flames higher, despite the fact that the flames were already two stories over their head.

"Who is that?" Jax asked trepidatiously.

"I can't tell," I said. "I wonder if it's the Black Witch. Sweets, we can't get too close with the car. Whoever that is will hear us. Park here. We're walking the rest of the way," I told everyone.

Holly's grip on my hand intensified. "We're getting *out?*"

"How are we supposed to know what's going on if we don't get out?" I asked her.

"Red's right. We can't drive any closer. We've got to get out," Alba agreed.

Sweets pulled the car over to the side of the road. "No slamming car doors," I hissed, gently easing my back passenger door open I shoved Holly's unwilling frame out the door first. Jax lurched out behind me, and the two of them clung to my arms like two children on their mother's leg. Sweets and Alba got out too, and the five of us made our way towards the roaring fire.

As we approached, I could hear the sound of a man's voice chanting near the fire, invoking the spirits. He had set up an outline around the perimeter of the fire made of sticks and twigs, and when his body turned slightly, we could immediately see that it was Oliver.

Holly leaned over to whisper in my ear, "It's Oliver!"

"Shh," I hissed back. Squeezing her hand tighter, we moved forward, protected by the shadows of a row of hemlock trees to our left. Silently we circled the fire, far enough from the outer perimeter of it that we wouldn't be visible. When we got to the back of the fire the outline of a girl strapped to a table, straining to free herself, became visible. With a heavy heart, I knew immediately he had found another virgin.

I reached in front of me and poked Alba. She turned, and I nodded towards the girl. "We've got to free her!" I whispered as quietly as I could.

Alba nodded. Silently the five of us crept forward, drawing strength from one another. My heart pounded furiously in my ears. Closer and closer we crept until finally we were crouched down low behind the table. I motioned silently to Sweets and Alba to untie her hands and the rest of us would untie her feet. As my hand touched the girl's foot, her head immediately shot off of the table and looked around with wild eyes at the five of us. She was gagged, and tears drenched her cheeks. Her dark brown hair was matted down behind her head and stuck to her cheeks in clumps.

I put a single finger to my lips. "Shh," I whispered

and pointed towards Oliver.

She nodded emphatically and leaned her head back onto the table, her body trembled with fear. Holly and Jax were first to free her feet, but Alba and Sweets struggled with her wrist cuffs. The knots were tighter and had less slack to work with.

Alba lifted her head up and whispered at the girl. "Pull on your hands. The rope is too tight. See if you can get it to stretch a little."

"I've tried," she cried. "The ropes won't budge."

"Well, well, well," we heard a voice call from beyond the fire. I peeked out around the side of the table to see Oliver approaching us. His eyes were wild, demonic almost. Fear paralyzed my arms and legs, and I froze where I was. But it was too late. He had seen Alba. "Don't be shy girls, come on out."

Alba, the bravest of our five, stood immediately with her hands on her hips – ready to battle him as necessary. "Stop what you're doing Oliver!"

"Oh, and just who intends to make me?" he sneered, combing one hand through his graying hair.

"I do," Alba said haughtily.

"And me!" Through no decision of my own, my legs forced me to stand, and my mouth spoke bravely.

"The two of you think you'll take me, do you?" He threw his head back and laughed.

"And us," said Jax bravely, standing up next to me with Holly and Sweets following her.

"This is amazing," he cooed. "Five little witches, gathered for me, which one shall I kill first, la-di-da-didee." He danced around in front of us like a deranged psychotic institute escapee.

"You're psychotic, Oliver," I said emotionlessly.

"I'm sorry, are you saying you think I'm crazy?"

"If the straight jacket fits," I deadpanned.

The wide smile on his face vanished as he moved towards me quickly. "I'll show you who's crazy!" With one hand he wrapped his grisly fingers around my neck, and lifted me off of my feet. I looked down at my feet while I felt the blood draining from my face.

"Mercy!" Jax hollered.

He had me lifted off of my feet so high, that I could see the edge of the table right by my shins. I lifted my legs and shoved off of the edge of the table with the tips of my toes and in one quick toss; I had flipped myself over backward. As his wrists twisted with my movement, he couldn't keep hold of my neck and I landed on my feet in a crouching position just beyond the table.

"You think *that* impresses me?" he sneered. "You'll have to do a lot more than *that* to impress me!"

I heard Jax giggle just then. "That impressed *me*."

"Oh, it did? Well, then maybe *you* should be the first to go!" he hollered, sending a lightning bolt of electrically charged energy towards her with one quick motion. Jax's reflexes worked quickly enough that she was able to dodge the shot and while he was focused on Jax, Alba took the opportunity to launch herself at him, sending him reeling down onto the ground, towards the fire.

While they wrestled, I sprung forward, working on the girl's ropes once again. "What's your name?" I asked quickly.

"Christine," she answered nervously. "Christine Brimsley. He-he-he's my youth group counselor."

"Christine, I am, I mean, I was friends with Morgan. My name is Mercy, and we're going to get you out of here."

Christine looked at me curiously but nodded. I worked quickly to loosen her ropes. Suddenly, I had an idea. "Christine, I have an idea to get these off, but it might hurt. Do you trust me?"

She nodded emphatically. "I trust you, Mercy."

"Alba, I need fire!" I hollered.

"Little busy here, Red," she hollered back while using her full weight and strength to keep Oliver down.

I cast a sideways glance towards Holly and Sweets who were standing frozen in the shadow of the table. "Girls, a little help over there?" I said, pointing at Alba.

Sweets nodded and shot forward, plopping herself down on Oliver's stomach with a thud while Holly squatted over his legs, pinning them down. Jax jumped up and rushed to help by grabbing his arms. "We've got him!" Sweets hollered to Alba. "Go help Mercy."

"You're sure?"

"Yes, go, hurry."

Alba jumped up and rushed to Christine and me. She cupped the knot in one hand and snapped the other hand's fingers and blew, shooting an instant spark towards the knot.

"Ow, ow, it's hot!" she cried.

"Pull, Christine. Break the ropes!"

Christine strained against the ropes as the fire burned through the knot quickly. The charred rope fell to the ground as Christine pulled her right arm free. Alba rushed around to do the same thing to her left.

"Hurry!" Jax called out while wrestling Oliver's wiry arms. "He's getting stronger!"

In no time, Christine's other arm was freed. Alba and I helped her off the table. "We're parked back there," I hollered at her. "Go to the car and stay there! You can't be here right now," I instructed.

Christine nodded and fled. Oliver arched his back to watch her go. "No! You can't do this!" he cried. "I need her!"

A sudden power surge filled his body, and he broke free of Jax's grip on his arms. He shoved Sweets off of his stomach roughly and then easily pulled his legs out of Holly's weak grasp. Oliver nimbly jumped to his feet.

"Not bad for a one-hundred-year-old guy, eh?" He laughed.

"What do we do Mercy?" Jax asked.

My brain was too panicked to think clearly. I didn't know what to do. I felt like we were out of options. I only wished we were further ahead in school to know some applicable spells.

"Thanks to you *witches*," he spat as if witches were a dirty word, "I've got to go retrieve my sacrificial lamb." He turned on his heel and began to walk towards where we had parked our car. I felt nauseous. We were out of options. He was too strong for us, and our minimal knowledge of magic wasn't enough.

"No!" Jax hollered. "Use me!"

My eyes flared as I spun around to look at Jax incredulously. "Jax, no!"

"It's ok, Mercy," she said quietly. "I can't let him hurt that girl."

Oliver stopped in his tracks with his back to us; slowly he began to turn around. "Use you? You're a witch. I can't use a witch in this spell."

Jax stepped towards him solemnly. "I'm not a witch."

His head cocked slightly to the right as he considered her. "But you're a student of SaraLynn Stone."

Jax nodded. "I am."

"But SaraLynn Stone doesn't take non-witches at her school," he insisted.

"She made an exception," Jax said quietly, staring him down.

He shook his head. "Why would SaraLynn Stone make an exception for *you*?" he asked, dumbfounded.

"Because she's my daughter!" we suddenly heard come from a voice behind Oliver.

CHAPTER TWENTY-THREE

Our heads collectively swiveled towards the voice. Sorceress Stone was walking towards us. My jaw dropped in awe.

"And my niece," said another voice. Behind Stone was a tall woman who looked very similar to her, but her hair was onyx black.

Our eyes flipped back to Jax, who looked like she just wanted to crawl into a hole and die of embarrassment now that her secret was revealed.

"BethAnn, I'm so glad you could make it!" Oliver gushed. "I've missed you my darling."

"Wait, so who is BethAnn again?" Holly whispered to us girls.

"It sounds like she's Sorceress Stone's sister," I whispered back.

"She's my aunt," Jax admitted. "I'm sorry I didn't tell

you girls. I-I-I couldn't."

"BethAnn, she's the one in the yearbook picture with Oliver?" Alba asked.

"I'm *so* confused," Sweets muttered. "I thought BethAnn was the Black Witch."

"I'll lay it all out there for you girls," Sorceress Stone announced. "Oliver is my sister's ex-boyfriend. After they broke up many many years ago, he became a different person. An evil person. So to bind him to a life of good versus an evil one, she put a curse on him. It took away the majority of his powers, leaving him with only enough magic to grow old gracefully and maybe make himself a sandwich. He is here tonight, outside of my sister's house on the Autumnal Equinox to sacrifice a virgin. He thinks he has found a spell to break the curse and retrieve his powers."

My sister's house? All of our eyes swung to BethAnn. Did this mean that Jax's aunt was the Black Witch? My jaw dropped, I couldn't believe it. Her face wasn't burned by acid. She wasn't an atrocious monster looking thing.

"Am I right, Oliver, dear?" the sorceress purred.

"You know me so well, SaraLynn" he stammered nervously, running another hand over the top of his head. "How did you know I'd be here?"

"Oh, I didn't know, though I should have, all the signs were there," the sorceress admitted, and then turned her gaze to stare directly at me. "It was really because of Mercy, here, that I was alerted to what was going on this evening."

"Me?" I asked, dumbfounded. I had no idea what she

was talking about.

"Your mother told me that it was you and your friends that freed my daughter from Evan and found Morgan's body. She told me that you all figured out that it was Oliver who killed Morgan because she was a virgin. Once I had those pieces of the puzzle, it didn't take much to figure out that you were going to pull a big stunt tonight. When BethAnn alerted me that someone had started a bonfire in the field next to her house, I knew who it was."

"My mother told you?" I asked, stunned. "But my mother is in Illinois!"

"She said she likes to call it – what did she say – Skitches? Skype for Witches?" Sorceress Stone laughed. "I thought that was pretty creative. Skitches…" she trailed off and let a little giggle escape.

"You can talk to her too?" I asked as more of a statement than a question.

"Mmmhmm, dear. I can talk to animals. I *am* a witch, you know."

"Glad that you've got this whole family reunion thing figured out," Oliver said, breaking our focus on each other to remind us what we were dealing with, "but I'm sorry to say, I've got work to do, so if you'll excuse me." Before anyone could object, he sent a stream of energy towards Jax, sending her reeling high into the sky above the flames of the fire and began chanting as he had been when we'd arrived.

Holly and Sweets screamed. I looked helplessly to Alba. Her eyes shamefully swung towards the ground.

Neither of us knew what to do.

"Girls, we're going to need your help. Focus your energy, concentrate on moving her body, and visualize Jax's feet touching the ground. To bring her down it will take all of us," she hollered, throwing her robed arms out to her sides, she extended her hand to me. Her sister took hold of one of her hands, and I took the one offered to me. I held my other hand out to Alba and quickly she took it, starting a chain reaction where Alba, Holly, and Sweets all joined hands. When Sweets took the Black Witch's hand, and the circle was complete, I felt the energy flowing between us.

Sorceress Stone closed her eyes as did her sister. I followed suit and did what she said, focusing my energy on Jax and visualizing her feet on the ground.

"No!" I heard Oliver holler. I peeked one eye open and saw Jax finally moving despite the electrical current he was still heaving towards her. "NO!"

She was away from the fire, finally hovering over the ground. We sat her down gently, flat on her back, but as we did, Oliver hurled a blast of energy towards BethAnn. "Curse you, *witch*," he spat.

The Black Witch held up her two flattened palms to meet the attack, and as she fired it back towards him, Sorceress Stone hurled a bolt of energy towards him, causing him to fly to the other side of the bonfire. The double sided attack lit up the night sky in one solid flash of light. Oliver fell into a crumpled heap as we saw flashing lights flying up the Black Witch's driveway in the distance. The wail of the Aspen Falls PD's sirens filled the night air.

The rest of the Witch Squad ran to Jax's side. "Jax, Jax, oh my god, are you alright?" Sweets asked as she got to her side first.

"Is she breathing?" I asked. Fear filled my whole body.

"I don't know," said Sweets.

"Move aside," the sorceress said from behind us. She rushed to her daughter's side and knelt down next to her. "JaclynRose, are you alright?"

I looked up at the other girls in surprise. "JaclynRose?" I mouthed.

"Mother! I told you not to call me that," said a raspy little voice from the ground.

Jax had her eyes open faintly, and she had a cross look on her face. Sorceress Stone let a tiny little smile escape her usually stony exterior.

"A little spit fire as usual," she said with eyes I thought looked a little damp around the edges. "You're going to be just fine. Girls, take care of her. I've got to go see to Oliver."

I nodded, looking down at Jax's tiny outline. "You're going to be alright JaclynRose," I teased.

"Shut up, Mercy. It's Jax. I'll run away again if you start calling me that," she said with a pout.

I crossed my heart with my finger. "I couldn't stand it if you did, Jax, never again, you have my word."

"Good," she said with a weak cough. "Help me up?"

We pulled her to her feet and walked towards Oliver and the flashing police lights.

"Looks like you were right," Detective Whitman said as we approached Oliver's lifeless body. "Oliver was Morgan's killer. Her family will be very thankful you caught him."

"What about Oliver, is he…" I began.

Detective Whitman nodded. "Yes, he's dead."

My shoulders finally began to loosen.

"You'll also find Christine Brimsley in our car," Alba told him.

He nodded and looked back towards the car. "We found her. She came running the minute the cruisers pulled into the driveway. You saved that poor girl's life. Thank you."

I smiled shyly, while Holly and Alba beamed with pride.

"You saved my daughter's life too," Sorceress Stone added. "I'm sorry I was so harsh on you. Girls come from far and wide and get in trouble very early in their college career. I make it a point to keep everyone in line, but maybe I take it a bit, too far. I'm sorry I made it impossible for you to come to me with your knowledge. Thank you for saving Jax. I don't know what I'd do with her."

We all looked at Jax who was beaming from ear to ear. "Thanks, Mom, I don't know what I'd do without you either."

Suddenly a thought occurred to me. I turned around in a circle. "Where did your aunt go?"

Sorceress Stone waved her hand dismissively. "She's not one for a crowd. She's gone back home."

"But…I don't understand…people say she's…" I began.

"Now is not the time or the place, Mercy, dear. It's been a long night, a long week, I suppose. Perhaps we should get the five of you back to campus. I'm sure a nice hot shower will do you all some good."

"And dessert, dessert will also do us some good," Sweets tossed in.

CHAPTER TWENTY-FOUR

Breakfast the next morning was certainly something to behold. The Witch Squad, as we were now being called by *everyone* at the Paranormal Institute, was subject to dozens of sets of interested eyes. It was all over school – we had solved the Morgan Hartford murder and saved Jax from Evan's evil wrongdoings. And we had most certainly saved a town girl from certain death. And best of all – *we'd met the Black Witch!*

I didn't know how excitingly grand that last part was myself. I mean BethAnn Stone certainly didn't *look* like one would think a Black Witch would look. I had to wonder if she was evil at all or if she was just the subject of a rumor mill a mile wide. While I wanted to ask Jax, I'd promised her that night that we'd save family stories for another day entirely. I'd also promised Jax, as had Holly, Sweets, and Alba that we'd keep her family lineage a secret just as we promised to keep Jax's lack of powers and her real name a secret as well.

One thing the Witch Squad could agree upon was that we definitely needed to learn more about witchcraft. If it hadn't been for my mother's meddling, Sorceress Stone, and the Black Witch's powers, we wouldn't have been able to stop Oliver on our own. Sorceress Stone guaranteed us that if we kept going to classes, by the end of our time at the Paranormal Institute, we'd have a much stronger grasp on the craft.

"We're like celebrities," Holly chirped excitedly.

"Except we're not," Alba grumbled into her ham and cheese omelet. "It's just weird having all of this attention."

I laughed. "Yeah, the last time I got this much attention, my entire chemistry class was watching out the window as I was being hauled off in cuffs in a squad car."

Holly, Jax, and Sweets looked at me in horror while Alba laughed.

"What? You've never had a troubled childhood? Sheesh, thought we were in a *no judging* circle here," I grumbled as I picked at my scrambled eggs.

Suddenly I heard the murmur of women's voices go from a subdued morning gossip session to a full out celebrity sighting buzz. I looked up to see what caused the sudden craze and saw the top of a cowboy hat moving through the crowd.

In seconds the bobbing hat had morphed into a full-on cowboy, complete with belt buckle, boots, and a country boy so hot he just about knocked my socks off.

"Howdy, Mercy Habernackle," he mockingly drawled

as he tipped his hat to me in front of the whole table and truly in front of the whole school.

I felt my face blush crimson red. "Howdy, Houston Brooks," I gave him a shy, cautious smile. "You're a little late for breakfast. Is there something I can help you with?"

"I've come to collect on your bill," he smirked.

"My bill?"

"I do believe you *owe me one*."

"I don't recall…" I began nervously.

"Ladies," he said without taking his hazel eyes off of mine. "What did Miss Habernackle here promise me?"

On cue, Holly giggled. "She said she owes you one."

Sweets nodded with an enormous smile on her face. "Yup! I was there. You owe him one, Mercy."

Alba nearly spit into her breakfast. "Ha, the man has a point, Red."

I covered my face with my hands; I could feel all the jealous eyes of the ladies in the courtyard burning on my face. I sucked in a deep breath and looked at Houston again. "Ok, fine. A deal is a deal. I promised I owe you one. What, pray tell, do I *owe* you?"

"I thought you'd never ask," he grinned. "I'd like to take you on a date tonight. 7:30 sharp. Wear something pretty – no sneakers. We're going somewhere nice."

I rolled my eyes playfully. "I'm afraid I can't go out with someone who won't let me wear my sneakers on a date." I laughed.

I heard Holly suck in her breath, causing me to relent slightly.

"There's a time and a place, Mercy Habernackle, and tonight, I intend to knock your socks off, so you might as well leave them at home."

"Fine. 7:30?"

"Yes, ma'am. I'll meet you in the courtyard," he said. "I'll look forward to it. Have a nice day. Ladies." He nodded his head at our table before turning on the heel of his cowboy boots and heading back to Warner Hall.

"Eeee," squealed Sweets. "I love it when I don't even have to cast a spell, and two people work out."

"Ha!" I harrumphed. "Work out? We're just going out on a date, and only because I owe him one! Now, if you'll excuse me, I need to go get my books ready for class. I'll talk to you ladies in class."

I quickly scampered away back towards Winston Hall and the safety of my dorm room. Before I got there, a familiar presence halted me at the bottom of the stairs.

"Morgan! You're back! I wondered if I'd ever see you again," I said, smiling at her ghost broadly.

"I had to come back. My parents are able to plan my funeral service now. I've been hanging with them all night. When they got the call telling them that Oliver was my killer and that he was dead, they felt so relieved. They cried, but they said they knew that I could be at peace now."

Her words filled my heart with a tremendous amount of joy, that I couldn't stop myself from smiling. "I'm so glad to hear that, Morgan."

"They were right, Mercy. I can be at peace now," she said, fingering the tiny necklace at her neck. Her spirit began to flicker in front of me, like an old black and white television program that needed the antenna adjusted.

"I think you're going, Morgan. I'll miss you," I said quickly before she disappeared.

"I'll miss you too, Mercy. I'll watch over my parents, tell them that someday. And that I love them very much," she said before her light flickered out entirely and just like that, Morgan was gone.

I smiled quietly to myself and stood staring at the place that she had been standing for several long seconds before continuing up to my dorm room where I was finally able to lean up against my closed door and let out the nervous breath I had been holding.

"What's with you?" I heard come from the window.

Sneaks was standing on the sill, surveying my body language. "Mom!" I hollered. "Quit spying!"

The cat jumped down off the sill onto my desk and curled her tail around her. "I'm hardly spying, Mercy. I'm trying to make sure you're alright after everything that just happened."

"Yes Mom, I'm fine. Thanks for sending Stone after us. There's no way we could have defeated Oliver without you. I need to work harder on my abilities. There's so much I don't know."

"That's why you're here, sweetie. To learn. I'm glad that's finally getting through to you. I can tell. College has been good for you already," she purred.

I suddenly wished she were actually standing in front of me so I could give her a big hug. Instead, I opted to pick up Sneaks and carry her to my bed where I curled up next to her and patted her soft black fur quietly. "I suppose it has been. It's been stressful, though. I'm looking forward to things calming down around here."

Mom hesitated for several long seconds. "Mercy, I know you want things to calm down, but there's something important I need to tell you. I have a secret that I've kept from you your whole life. I was going to take this secret to my grave, but something has changed, and now I feel that I must warn you."

My heart dropped. I didn't know if I could handle something else after everything we'd just been through. "Mom, you're scaring me," I said, nervously nibbling at my fingernails.

"When I was young. Younger than you are now, I did something really stupid," she admitted.

My mind raced. What could she possibly have done that she'd have the need to tell me right now? "Ok…?" I sucked in a deep breath and held it.

"I was young and stupid. And I met someone. He was older and extremely handsome, and he was a wizard. The magic that that man could do! Oh, he was amazing. And I was smitten, I'd found the love of my life! I wanted to run off with him and marry him, but my mother wouldn't let me. She didn't like that he was older and worldlier than I and she didn't like that he was so powerful. So, on my 17th birthday, she performed a binding spell. She cursed us both so that we would never be able to speak to each other again. For months I cried and cried and ignored everything and everyone around me."

"Mom, why are you tell me all of this?" I asked her nervously.

"And one day, I woke up feeling very strange. I didn't know what was happening, and I went to my mother. I was still angry with her about binding me, but I was also scared and I didn't have anyone else to turn to. My stomach was cramping horribly, and I felt sick like I'd never felt before. She took me to the hospital where it was discovered that I was pregnant, Mercy."

I felt like my heart stopped beating. I held my breath again, waiting for her to finish her story.

"And the baby was coming. At any moment, I'd deliver a child. My mother was furious with me. How had I not known? How had *she* not known? We'd all missed the signs. But a baby was coming. That day, I'll never forget it; I gave birth to a son."

A son, I had a brother?!

"He was beautiful, Mercy. He had a shock of midnight black hair and tiny dimples formed in his cheeks when he cried. He looked just like his father. The minute my mother saw him and saw how he resembled his father, she took him from me. Just like that," I could hear my mother sniffling, holding back her tears. "She plucked him from my arms and took him. She told me she was taking him to the nursery so that they could watch over him and I could get some sleep. Of course, I protested, I wanted to hold my son. The son that the man I was in love with had given me, but my mother refused, insisting I get some sleep and she would bring him back later in the day."

"What happened to him?" I asked in a hushed tone, scared to hear what had happened to my brother.

"Your dear old granny, the one you love so much, never brought my son back. When I woke up, my mother was gone. I asked the nurse to bring me my baby. She went to the nursery and came back and said that my mother had given him up for adoption. I argued that I hadn't consented to such a thing, but because I wasn't 18 yet, she was my legal guardian and had the right to give my baby away without my permission."

I sucked in my breath. I couldn't believe it, how could my dear, sweet granny have done such a wicked thing? My poor mother! What she'd gone through! I couldn't imagine.

"And so, that was it, Mercy. I went home from the hospital the next day without my son. For a year I cried and begged and pleaded for my mother to tell me where my son was, to let me have him, let me see him. She refused day after day. And so finally, the begging and the pleading died down. I had to move on with my life. Once my son was a year old, I knew that I'd only be interfering in his life if I ever sought him out. And so I let him go."

I sniffed back the sobs that were racking my body. "Mom, why are you telling me this now?"

"He's come to find me, Mercy. Your brother, he found me. He was waiting for me when I came home from delivering you to college. I didn't want to tell you because you were so preoccupied this week, but he wants to meet you Mercy. The minute he found out he had a sister, he asked to meet you."

"I have a brother that wants to meet me?" I asked. My mind was in a state of shock.

"Yes. And he's on his way to see you. He should be there soon, today or tomorrow. I need to warn you. He's special Mercy, very special. You must promise me that you'll keep an eye on him at all times."

"How is he special?" I asked nervously.

"You'll see Mercy. Just promise me that you'll keep an eye on him."

I nodded my head. With one solemn vow, I changed the course of my life forever, "I promise Mother."

ABOUT THE AUTHOR

M.Z. grew up in a small town in Nebraska. She is married and together she and her husband have four daughters, two sons, and one obese cat.

M.Z. is an avid gardener and DIY enthusiast. In her spare time she enjoys reading and watching football games.

She and her family currently reside in South Dakota.

Made in the USA
Middletown, DE
15 May 2017